# PRAISE FOR
# GAME CHANGER

An Amazon Best Book of the Month

A 2019 YALSA Top Ten Quick Pick for Reluctant Young Adult Readers

A Junior Library Guild Premier Selection

Dorothy Canfield Fisher Book Award Nominee

Kentucky Bluegrass Awards Master List for Grades 6-8

Louisiana Young Readers' Choice Award Nominee

Maine Student Book Award Nominee

Maryland Black-Eyed Susan Book Award Nominee

Rhode Island Middle School Book Award Nominee

TAYSHAS Reading List

Lone Star Reading List

Virginia Readers' Choice Nominee

Pennsylvania Young Readers Choice Award Nominee

Wyoming Soaring Eagle Book Award Nominee

Colorado Children's Book Award Finalist

Florida Sunshine State Young Readers List

Delaware Diamonds Secondary Titles List

Iowa Teen Award Nominee

# GAME CHANGER

## TOMMY GREENWALD

AMULET BOOKS

NEW YORK

For Jack, Joe, and Charlie

The Library of Congress has cataloged the hardcover edition as follows:
Names: Greenwald, Tom, 1962- author.
Title: Game changer / by Tommy Greenwald.
Description: New York : Amulet Books, 2018. | Summary: While thirteen-year-old Teddy fights for his life after a football injury at training camp, his friends and family gather to support him and discuss events leading to his coma. Told through dialogue, text messages, newspaper articles, transcripts, an online forum, and Teddy's inner thoughts.
Identifiers: LCCN 2017055217 | ISBN 9781419731433 (hardcover with jacket)
Subjects: | CYAC: Football—Fiction. | Sports injuries—Fiction. | Coma—Fiction. | Hazing—Fiction. | Family problems—Fiction.
Classification: LCC PZ7.G8523 Gam 2018 | DDC [Fic]—dc23

Paperback ISBN 978-1-4197-3697-1

Text copyright © 2018 Tommy Greenwald
Jacket illustrations copyright © 2018 Neil Swabb
Book design by Melissa J. Barrett

Printed and bound in U.S.A.
10 9 8 7 6 5 4 3 2 1

Amulet Books are available at special discounts when purchased in quantity for premiums and promotions as well as fundraising or educational use. Special editions can also be created to specification. For details, contact specialsales@abramsbooks.com or the address below.

Amulet Books® is a registered trademark of Harry N. Abrams, Inc.

ABRAMS The Art of Books
195 Broadway, New York, NY 10007
abramsbooks.com

**game changer** *n*: an event, idea, or procedure that effects a significant shift in the current manner of doing or thinking about something

# WINNING THE

# WALTHORNE WAY

WE ARE THE WALTHORNE WILDCATS.

WE WIN AS A TEAM.

WE LOSE AS A TEAM.

WE WORK TOGETHER.

WE PLAY TOGETHER.

WE FIGHT TOGETHER.

WE TRUST ONE ANOTHER.

WE PROTECT ONE ANOTHER.

WE SUPPORT ONE  ANOTHER.

WE DEFEND ONE ANOTHER.

WE RESPECT ONE ANOTHER.

NO ONE IS ALONE ON THE TEAM.

NO ONE IS BIGGER THAN THE TEAM.

NO ONE COMES BETWEEN YOU AND THE TEAM.

WE ARE THE WALTHORNE WILDCATS.

# High Expectations for Walthorne Football This Season

In a tradition that signals the end of summer almost as much as back-to-school sales and falling leaves, the Walthorne High School Wildcats football program opened their preseason training camp this morning.

More than one hundred student-athletes, from incoming freshmen to returning varsity stars, gathered together at Wildcat Stadium, participating in what Coach Louis Bizetti called "the first step in our long journey together." Coach Bizetti, the Hall of Fame legend who is beginning his sixteenth season leading the Wildcats, already has three state titles under his belt and thinks this year could make four. "I'm really excited about our chances," he said. "We've got a ton of talent on this team, and I expect to go a long way."

Captain Will Burdeen, a senior all-state running back and defensive back, echoed his coach's sentiments. "We've got some great kids, and I'm really excited," said Will, during morning stretching. "This camp will give the returning players a head start on achieving our goals while working the new kids in and getting them pumped up about joining our amazing program."

Walthorne's varsity season begins Friday night, September 16, with a home game against Ramsdale High School. The game is already sold out, but there is a standby list for cancellations—visit WalthorneWildcats.com for more information.

# PART ONE

FRIDAY, AUGUST 26

5:43 PM


## HOSPITAL ADMITTANCE REPORT


EDWARD YOUNGBLOOD

13-YEAR-OLD MALE, HEAD TRAUMA.

POSSIBLE INTRACRANIAL BLEED.

NO EXTERNAL INJURIES.

COMATOSE, NEEDS TOTAL RESPIRATORY CARE.


**CONDITION: CRITICAL**

## INSIDE

*Light in the darkness*

*Circles without shape*

*Colors I can't see*

*Memories I can't feel*

*Voices but no words*

*Thoughts but no meaning*

*Come on, Eden, let's do this*

*Don't be soft*

*Can you hit somebody?*

*Show me you can hit somebody*

*Eden*

*Eden, come on*

*Come on*

*Eden*

*I'm*

*I didn't*

*Don't be a girl*

*This wasn't*

*I'm falling*

*I'm falling*

*I'm*

*I'm*

*Is it raining?*

GUYS
JUST CHECKING IN TO MAKE SURE
EVERYONE HAS THE LATEST INFO

INCOMING FRESHMAN TED YOUNGBLOOD IS IN THE
HOSPITAL FROM THAT HIT HE TOOK AT CAMP TODAY

IT'S PRETTY BAD, NOT SURE HOW BAD YET
BUT I HEARD HE'S STILL UNCONSCIOUS

IT SUCKS

EVEN THOUGH THESE THINGS HAPPEN IN
FOOTBALL SOMETIMES IT TOTALLY SUCKS

I WANT TO MAKE SURE EVERYONE IS DOING OKAY

EVERYONE ON THE TEAM NEEDS TO
KEEP THEIR HEADS IN THE GAME

BE STRONG AND STICK TOGETHER

WE'RE A TEAM AND WE'LL ALWAYS BE A TEAM

NEVER FORGET THAT GUYS!

IF I HEAR ANYTHING ELSE I'LL
UPDATE ON THIS THREAD

OTHERWISE SEE EVERYONE AT
PRACTICE MONDAY 8AM SHARP

## DR. SPARKS

Mr. and Mrs. Youngblood

I want you to know your son is in the best hands

He's getting the finest care

The very best care

The most important thing for him is rest

So his brain can heal

And he needs to know you're there

It's important to talk to him

He can hear you, I promise

He is listening

Not in the traditional sense, of course

And we can't expect any sort of response just yet

But he can hear every word you say

It's very important to keep talking to him

One person at a time is best

Multiple voices can be too much

We don't want to overwhelm him

But he needs to be stimulated

Stay positive and strong

Try not to sound upset or scared

Talk about anything you want, but stay upbeat

He will get through this as long as you're right there with him

Remember

Every word counts.


**MOM**

Honey

Teddy

Can you feel my hand?

Squeeze my hand if you can feel it

Squeeze it, honey

Okay, maybe later

I

Am I too close?

I'm going to sit

I'll sit here, okay?

I stopped by the house and picked up a bunch of your things

Some posters and your favorite pj's and other stuff

But I forgot your pillow

I'm so mad I forgot your pillow

I texted Dad

He just left to pick up Janey, so I asked him to get it

I'm going to wash the pillowcase

Get it nice and soft just the way you like it

I know how much you love that pillow

I would get it myself, but I don't want to leave you right now

I want to stay right here

I'm going to stay right here

I love you so much

I'm here

I'm not going anywhere, sweetheart

I'm never going anywhere again

I'm back

I'm here

I'm back for good.

**DAD**

Hey

Hey, bud

How's my guy?

How's my man?

You look great, Teddy

You look really good

You really do

I'm not just saying that

You look strong

Okay, so

Uh

I know you saw Mom

She hasn't been

You know

It's been a while, kiddo

But she loves you very much

More than anything in this world

She only wants to see you get better

We all need to be a family right now

Hey, look what I found

I guess I had it in the office

One of your first game balls

Oh man, remember?

The sixth-grade championship a few years back?

That was some game

You made that goal line tackle and the whole team jumped on you

Crowd going nuts

That's what it's all about

Remember they used to call you the "game changer"?

Because you were always the one who made the difference

Man was I proud

Oh yeah

I brought your speakers

You can blast your music as loud as you want

So

Oh man

You'll be just fine, Teddy

I know you will

You're such a tough kid

So strong and tough

You look really great, though, you really do

Oh shoot

I got Mom's text about the pillow, but I forgot to bring it

I better go get it

Okay, kiddo

Somebody wants to say hi

Go ahead, honey

Don't be afraid

Go ahead.

**JANEY**

Hey, Teddy

Um

Hi

Are you

Are you doing okay?

Ugh

That was stupid

So

Yeah, no

They said

They said just talk to you like I guess I would talk to you any other day, right?

Okay, so

I can't believe Dad forgot your pillow. Of course that turned into a whole thing, what else is new? But anyway, Dad is going back to the house to get it. It's weird to see Mom and Dad together. Like, it's the same, but different. Your hair is super dirty by the way. You're lucky you can't see it. I mean, obviously you're not, but you are. What a mess, somebody should totally wash it for you, it's like really greasy, and like, you would be so mad if you saw your hair right now, you would be like, so mad if you could see yourself. You know how you stare at yourself in the mirror all the time and I yell at you because I need the bathroom

Maybe Dad can get the nurse to wash it

I didn't know they had men nurses

Or I guess I knew they did, but I don't think I've ever met one before

Do you want me to check your texts? Or Dad can I guess

Alec texted me, he said he's coming

He got a text from Camille, she is going to come see you too, with her dad

I guess a lot of people already heard about what happened, like the whole town has heard already, and everybody feels horrible, all the kids in your grade and stuff, they're all kind of freaking out, especially the boys on the football team, I'm sure you know that already

Alec sounded so scared

Oh wait, I forgot Mom said I shouldn't talk about that stuff

Uh

Yeah, so, I'll see you tomorrow, okay?

Night, Teddy

Please come home

Wash that hair though, okay?

9:09 PM
ALEC

ETHAN

ETHAN ARE YOU THERE

DUDE WHAT'S GOING ON

PLS TEXT ME BACK

PEOPLE WANT TO KNOW HOW U R DOING

JUST MKING SURE YOU'RE OKAY

LET ME KNOW IF YOU WANT TO TALK ABOUT IT

SERIOUSLY ETHAN TEXT ME BACK OKAY??

**Camille** I don't know if everyone heard but Teddy Youngblood was hurt today at football preseason camp. He is in the hospital and I'm not sure how serious it is but I think it's pretty serious because my dad has been on the phone with different people for hours and it seems like it's bad. I have been crying all night I feel like I have no more tears left. As soon as I have more information from my dad I will let everyone know and if anybody knows anything else they should share it too. I'm so scared.

👍 37

Like · Reply

## NURSE RICKY

Hello there, Mr. Edward Youngblood

I like that name by the way

I really do

Anyway

I'm Nurse Ricky

But you can call me just Ricky

I'll be looking after you during your stay here with us

My job is to make your visit as comfortable as possible

So if there's anything you need, please don't hesitate to holler

Sound good?

Your family is here and they love you very much

That's a good-looking family you got there by the way

Not too shabby

But it's almost bedtime

Time to dream

*Forget your troubles, come on get happy*
*We're gonna wipe all your cares away*

You know that song?

Of course not

It's way before your time

It's way before *my* time

You just get your rest, okay?

So your kid sister was giving me a hard time about not washing your hair

Feisty little thing, isn't she?

Gotta keep on her good side, yes I do

So let's do this

Here, let me lift you up just a little

Fix this mop up once and for all

There we go

There we are

That feels better, right?

*That's the way uh-huh uh-huh*
*I like it uh-huh uh-huh*
*That's the way I like it*

You know that song?

You don't know that one either?

We need to educate you in the ways of music

Yup, there we go

This oughta make your sister happy

Tough little cookie, that one

Tomorrow we're going to give you a bath

Deal?

Okay good, you just get your rest

My goodness you're just a child

They're just children

Just babies

Why is this world getting so crazy?

## MOM

Sweetie

Honey

Tomorrow we start to fight our way back

We're gonna fight, honey

The doctor said you could have a few more visitors

Friends and family only though

I guess the team wants to come

The boys who were there

They're still shocked of course

But they were hoping to see you to make sure you're okay

That you're gonna be okay

And I guess the high school coach who runs the camp

Coach Bizetti I think his name is

He called Dad

He wants to come by too

Supposedly he's a legend around here, like a god or something

We all know how nuts this town is about football, right?

Don't worry though, I won't embarrass you by telling him how I
really feel

I would never do that to you

Anyway, he wants to come say hi

Dad said the coach told him you're a great player

Which is very nice, but honestly I'm more interested in finding out what happened

He needs to tell us exactly what happened

We have gotten so many calls and texts from people wanting to come

Everyone wants to see you, Teddy

Everyone wants to see you get better

But no one more than me and Janey, and Daddy

I'm so

I still can't believe this

But if anyone can handle it, it's you

So it's time for bed I guess

But first I just

I just need to tell you something, Teddy

I need to tell you that I wish I'd been here

I just

I really do

So okay, sleep well, honey

I'm so glad Dad got your pillow

I'll be right here if you need me

Right next to you

Right here.

10:32 PM
ETHAN

HEY ALEC

THANKS FOR TEXTING BUT I'M OKAY

I DON'T REALLY FEEL LIKE
TALKING ABOUT IT THOUGH

MY PARENTS ARE MAKING ME
TALK TO SOME GUY TOMORROW

BUT WHATEVER

THANKS FOR CHECKING IN

10:49 PM

WILL

YO ETHAN THIS IS WILL

CAPTAIN OF VARSITY

YOUR BUDDY ALEX GAVE ME YOUR NUMBER

HE SAID YOU TEXTED HIM A FEW MINUTES AGO

I HOPE YOU'RE OKAY

SO A LOT OF KIDS FROM CAMP ARE GONNA BE TALKING TO THESE PEOPLE FROM SCHOOL

THERAPISTS OR SOMETHING

I'M SURE YOU ARE TOO RIGHT?

JUST WANT TO MAKE SURE YOU'RE COOL

THANKS

TODAY 10:54 PM

HEY ETHAN THIS IS WILL AGAIN

JUST HIT ME BACK TO LET ME KNOW YOU GOT MY LAST TEXT

THANKS

TODAY 11:01 PM

ETHAN YOU THERE?

I HOPE YOU'RE NOT MAD OR UPSET AT WHAT I SAID TO YOU AT CAMP TODAY

WE WERE ALL A LITTLE FREAKED OUT BECAUSE OF WHAT HAPPENED

I HOPE IT DIDN'T SOUND LIKE I WAS BLAMING YOU, IT'S NOBODY'S FAULT, REMEMBER THAT

TODAY 11:22 PM

YOU DON'T HAVE TO TEXT ME BACK

NP I GET IT

STAY COOL TOMORROW

HOPE IT GOES OKAY

SATURDAY, AUGUST 27

8:45 AM

**PATIENT REPORT**

MODEST IMPROVEMENT.

MRI REVEALS SWELLING OF THE BRAIN.

REMAINS IN A COMATOSE STATE.

BREATHING WITH ASSISTANCE.

**CONDITION: CRITICAL**

MR. RASHAD:    Hi Ethan, I'm Mr. Rashad. It's good to meet you.

ETHAN:    You too.

MR. RASHAD:    So. Please, take a seat, make yourself comfortable. Did you want to ask me anything before we get started?

ETHAN:    Not really.

MR. RASHAD:    Okay fine. I can tell you a little bit about myself, if you want.

ETHAN:    Yeah, sure.

MR. RASHAD:    Well, I work for the town of Walthorne as a therapist in the education department, where I've been for twelve years. I love working with kids, talking to kids like you about anything and everything. And just so you know, I'm a huge football fan. Played it in high school, still watch it every weekend. Greatest game in the

world, in my opinion. What happened
to your teammate is a tragedy, in so
many ways.

ETHAN:         Yup.

MR. RASHAD:    So, right—that's pretty much my story,
               unless you have any questions.

ETHAN:         Nope.

MR. RASHAD:    Okay, great.

ETHAN:         Actually, why are you tape-recording
               this?

MR. RASHAD:    Good question. Basically, I'd rather
               talk to you without the distraction
               of having to take detailed notes
               the whole time, and the recordings
               help me when I need to refer back
               to the session. But if it makes you
               uncomfortable, I can certainly take
               notes instead.

ETHAN:         No, it's fine.

MR. RASHAD:    And Ethan, I just want to make sure
               you realize that you don't have to

do this at all, if you don't want to.
It's standard procedure to talk to
kids who witness something like this,
and your parents thought it might be
a good idea. None of us ever knows
quite how we're going to respond to a
traumatic event, and it's important to
be aware of what might happen. And if
you want one or both of your parents
to be with us when we talk, that's fine
too. Totally up to you. Good so far?

ETHAN:          Sure, yeah.

MR. RASHAD:     Okay, great.

ETHAN:          So you're not, like, a cop or
                something?

MR. RASHAD:     A cop? Oh no, no no, nothing like
                that. Like I said, I'm a therapist
                with the school system. Did you think
                I was with the police?

ETHAN:          I wasn't sure.

MR. RASHAD:     This has nothing to do with the police.
                No one did anything wrong. This was a
                terrible injury, a student was badly

hurt, and we're just checking in with the kids to make sure everyone is doing okay. That's the deal.

ETHAN:          Right. Well, I'm doing fine.

MR. RASHAD:     Great.

ETHAN:          So you're talking to other kids?

MR. RASHAD:     That's right, my colleagues and I are hoping to talk to as many of you all as possible.

ETHAN:          Uh-huh.

MR. RASHAD:     It's really just about helping you and your teammates deal with whatever you might be going through.

ETHAN:          Okay. A lot of them aren't really my teammates though, like the older kids. I'm not even in high school yet.

MR. RASHAD:     Got it. So, should we jump in? Do you want to talk about what happened?

ETHAN:          Well, I mean, that's the thing. Nothing really happened.

MR. RASHAD:    Well then, how about we talk a little about when Edward got injured—what you were feeling, how you reacted, that kind of thing.

ETHAN:    I told my parents ten times. The Rookie Rumble ended and Teddy collapsed. I don't really remember anything else.

MR. RASHAD:    The Rookie Rumble?

ETHAN:    Yeah. That's what they call the scrimmage on the last day of preseason camp. It's just for incoming freshmen.

MR. RASHAD:    Ah, got it. But Edward didn't collapse during the scrimmage? He collapsed right after?

ETHAN:    Everyone calls him Teddy. Yeah, right after, I guess. Doesn't that happen sometimes though, with like, concussions and stuff? Like, a delayed reaction or something?

MR. RASHAD:    I'll leave that answer to the medical professionals, but as far as I know, it's possible, yes.

ETHAN:          So then yeah, I guess that's what
                happened.

MR. RASHAD:     So you don't remember how you felt, or
                how you reacted, when you saw Teddy
                collapse?

ETHAN:          I was shocked. Like, in shock, I
                guess. This kid who's an awesome
                athlete and loves football more than
                anything in the world was lying on
                the ground unconscious right next to
                me. Like, who wouldn't freak out, you
                know?

MR. RASHAD:     I completely understand. What about in
                terms of how you feel about football?
                Do you like playing? Does this make
                you feel differently about the sport
                at all?

ETHAN:          I love football. It's always been my
                favorite sport. I mean, it's a little
                different now, I guess.

MR. RASHAD:     Different how?

ETHAN:          Well, for one thing, I used to be one
                of the best players, but not anymore.

For a while, I was one of the bigger kids in my grade, but then I stopped growing and now I'm pretty small.

MR. RASHAD: Ah. Yeah, well, unfortunately size matters in football, that's for sure. It's a dangerous enough sport as it is.

ETHAN: Yeah, I guess.

MR. RASHAD: Have you ever gotten injured playing football?

ETHAN: I—yeah, once, in like fifth grade or something. I sprained my ankle. Not that bad though.

MR. RASHAD: You've been lucky. You probably know this already, but a lot of people are starting to think football is too dangerous and kids shouldn't be allowed to play. Especially kids your age and younger. It's an ongoing discussion among coaches, educators, and parents.

ETHAN: I guess.

MR. RASHAD: But you think you want to play in high school?

ETHAN:          Being on the high school team is
                pretty much all I've thought about
                since forever.

MR. RASHAD:     Yeah, I get that. Being part of a
                team, part of something bigger than
                yourself, is one of the greatest
                things in life.

ETHAN:          Yeah.

MR. RASHAD:     Are you and Teddy friends?

ETHAN:          Everyone is friends with Teddy. He's
                like, the best athlete in the grade,
                pretty much.

MR. RASHAD:     It must have been so hard to see your
                friend so terribly hurt.

ETHAN:          He's—
                Is he going to be okay?
                He's going to be okay, right?

MR. RASHAD:     I hope so, Ethan. We all hope so.

## INSIDE

*I love the game*

*The shapes*

*The bodies*

*The grunts*

*I love having the one thing everyone else wants*

*I love running to daylight*

*Shifting*

*Escaping*

*I love knowing they're coming*

*I love bracing myself*

*I love getting hit*

*I love falling*

*I love the pain*

*It hurts*

*It hurts so bad*

*And it's the greatest feeling in the world.*

## DAD

Hey, buddy

Whoa, look at you

You look great

Good night's sleep?

Good dreams?

What's—

You look like you got some rest

And your hair's all washed

Man, you are a heartbreaker, buddy boy

Man

Big day today

Gonna be a good day

And hey, Coach Bizetti called me again this morning

He feels so terrible about what happened

Absolutely heartbroken

He said you would have been a terrific football player

Incredible potential

I said "Hey, let's not rule anything out, okay?"

Stranger things have happened, right?

But yeah

I mean I know you playing again is a long shot

But you never know

So anyway, this coach

He told me he has a daughter, Camille, who knows you?

He said she's having a really hard time with this

She's probably crazy about you, like all the girls, huh?

My son, the ladies' man

Anyway

The coach is helping to organize some sort of event for tonight, up at the high school, so people can come together and support you and pray for you

I bet the whole town is going to show up

This guy seems like a terrific coach who really cares about his kids

He was telling me about all the precautions they have in place

They take the safety of the players really seriously

The equipment is the best

State-of-the-art helmets

That's why this is so weird

I told him this wasn't anyone's fault

How could we know what would happen?

A fluke, just a horrible fluky thing

He seems like a good man

Anyway

Oh hey, guess what? Nana is coming to see you today

She can't wait to see you

Is the temperature good in here?

I know how cold you like your room

You got that from me

We used to argue about that all the time

Me and your mom

She was always cold, I was always hot

She would have piles of blankets on top of her and I would be
sweating and opening all the windows

It was amazing how different we were

We were so different

Not that that explains what happened, but anyway

It's pretty hot in here

I'll talk to someone about the AC

Oh, we got your class schedule, it looks good

First year of high school, Teddy

I'm jealous

Being a kid, that's really so awesome

You're going to have a blast.

## JANEY

Oh wow, Teddy, you look so much better

I guess now it makes sense that Camille likes you

Even though you're a totally annoying older brother almost all the time

I promise not to tell her that

Not yet anyway

Wait, what did I want to tell you? Oh yeah

I wanted to bring Ollie but Dad said I couldn't, so instead I brought this picture of him, which I'm going to leave next to your bed because I bet you miss him a lot. As much as he misses you probably. Last night, he was so funny. We got him this new toy that has like nine squeaks in it, and after he destroyed one squeak, he would go on to the next one, it took him about an hour to destroy the whole toy, which Dad said is a record for him. The house was so quiet except for Nana talking on the phone and Ollie squeaking his toy. Dad said he doesn't like buying toys because they're such a waste of money, but I said Ollie loves them so much even though they don't last very long. Mom used to say the same thing, so tonight I'm going to order some more toys online. And when Dad came home, he smiled at Ollie, and it was the first time I saw him smile in a while

Tonight I'm going to Mom's, we're ordering Chinese

I know, can you believe it?

I just asked and she said yes

But don't worry, I'll save you some, I promise

I have to go to soccer, but I'll be back later

Wake up soon, Teddy

Please

Ollie misses you and I miss you

Even though you're annoying

Ha

Just kidding

Come home, okay?

**MOM**

Hi, honey

Did you sleep okay?

Was the pillow okay?

I washed the pillowcase again last night

I don't mean to obsess about the pillow, but I can't help it, I remember it like it was yesterday

Do you remember?

You were six years old and I got you a new pillow, and I walked into your room the next morning and found it on the floor, and I asked you why and you said, "I want my old pillow," which I was just about to throw out because it was so ratty and old, and to this day you've never let me replace that pillow. And you hated all the pillowcases too, remember? Because they were too itchy? Every night, I'd put a new pillowcase on your pillow, and every night, you'd take it right off, so I searched and searched for the perfect pillowcase until finally three years ago I found it. I'll never forget coming into your room the next morning and you were sleeping and the pillowcase was still on your pillow and I swear to God it was like a miracle

Anyway, they brought a bed in for me

More of a cot, really, but it's pretty comfortable

Can you smell my coffee?

You used to love the smell of coffee

I'm going to wash up before the doctor gets here

I'll be right back

I'll be right here if you need anything

I'll be right here.

## DR. SPARKS

Well hello there, Teddy

Nice to see you

Just need to check a few things

Will only take a minute

Good

Terrific

You're a strong young man and you're doing very well

You're in fine shape

Football shape, I believe they call it

I bet you hit that hole hard, huh

Impressed by the lingo?

Don't be so shocked

I'm a big football fan, especially college football

My dad played in college, and he'll tell anyone who will listen all about it, too

My brothers played in high school

I played a little field hockey myself

There's nothing like being part of a team

I really do miss it

I know your teammates are excited to get you back

They want you with them

When you're on a team, you'll always be part of that team

The important thing for now is to get plenty of rest

We're taking very good care of you, that's a promise

And your family is here and they love you

I look forward to talking with you

You seem like a fine young man

Get some rest.

Saturday at 11:13 am

**Camille** PAGE FOR TEDDY!!!!

Please like this page!!!

Teddy Youngblood was hurt at football yesterday

He has a head injury and it's serious

Teddy and his family are in all of our thoughts

Also there is a service tonight at the high school

Please come so we can be together

Please use this page to share any thoughts you have about Teddy

As we pray for him to make a full recovery

Please pray for Teddy!!!

 27

Like · Reply

Saturday at 11:20 am

**Emily** Camille I am so upset. Teddy please please be okay I am praying for you so hard

20

Like · Reply

Saturday at 11:39 am

**Will** Hey Camille and everyone, my name is Will Burdeen and I'm the captain of the high school football varsity. On behalf of the team I just want to say how much we are all pulling for Teddy, he's a really good kid and a great football player, we know he'll pull through and we can't wait to see him back on the field.

 29

Like · Reply

Saturday at 11:47 am

**James** I agree with what Will said, Teddy is a great athlete and a tough competitor and he's going to make a great Walthorne Wildcat football player someday.

👍 14

Like · Reply

Saturday at 12:08 pm

**Frankie** That would be amazing but I don't think Teddy is going to make a great football player someday, or any day. If he has a really bad head injury then his playing days are over, unless he and his family have a death wish or something

👍 2

Like · Reply

Saturday at 12:39 pm

**Camille** Hi Frankie, I don't know you but just fyi this page is not meant for negative comments, it's to post thoughts about Teddy and pray for his recovery.

👍 16

Like · Reply

Saturday at 12:43 pm

**Clea** This is so sad. How did it happen? Does anyone know?

👍 4

Like · Reply

Saturday at 12:44 pm

**Darren** What do you mean? I think it was just a terrible football injury, right? Why, did you hear something else?

Like · Reply

Saturday at 12:51 pm

**Clea** I don't know, nothing I guess, I thought I heard that maybe it was more complicated than just a regular injury, but I mean I have no idea of course

Like · Reply

Saturday at 12:54 pm

**Jackie** Wow really, where did you hear that?

Like · Reply

Saturday at 12:57 pm

**Camille** Guys don't. Seriously this isn't about that. Just please pray for Teddy which would be so amazing and helpful. Thank you!! Think positive!!! ☺

14

Like · Reply

Direct message from Will

Saturday at 1:12 pm

Hey alex

You are best friends with teddy right?

Let me know how you're doing with all this

Coach Bizetti and the team want you to know that you
 don't have to worry about football right now

None of us are thinking about any of that

We just want teddy to get better

And remember we're a team

We stick together

Also if you hear from that kid ethan let me know cool?

Let me know if you need anything okay thx

Saturday at 1:22 pm

Okay i will
Thx for checking in

**MOM**

Honey, Alec is here

He's outside with his parents

He is brave to come here

It says a lot

He's a real friend

It's not easy

We're going to let him see you for a few minutes

He just really wants to say hi

The doctors think it's okay

A good idea, even if just for a few minutes

He really wants to see you, and I bet you want to see him too

Hold on okay?


**ALEC**

Hey

Uh, hey

So, like

How are you doing?

They treating you okay in here?

I

Yeah, so

You got a window

That's cool

The view is pretty good

That nurse is pretty weird

Funny though

I never met a guy nurse before

I bet the food sucks, huh?

Can you

You probably can't eat yet

So yeah

Camille started this group online

Which was really awesome

But then right away it got a little weird because a few people
started talking about how it happened

You know, like, was it really just a football injury or not

But Camille was like, shut up, that is so inappropriate

So I heard too that the varsity might cancel their first couple of
games

Or even the whole season

One of the captains DM'd me

That kid Will

He keeps calling me Alex, which is pretty funny

I'm too nervous to correct him though

Anyway he said, uh

He said that Coach Bizetti told him we shouldn't be thinking about football right now

Which is

Which is, uh

To be honest I don't know if I ever want to think about football again

I mean

I always loved being out there with you and the guys and stuff

And sometimes it was so awesome, like I totally remember the first time I ever scored a touchdown, in fourth grade. I was about to get tackled but you threw this amazing block and I just barely made it into the end zone, and you were the first kid there. You picked me up and gave me this massive hug and we yelled at the top of our lungs and it was so great

I'll never forget it

But now it's like, I don't know

I just

I'm not that into it anymore

I haven't been for a while

I didn't want to tell you because you're my best friend and I know how much you love it

But, like

My parents are saying there's no way you're going to be able to play again, like, ever

And I definitely don't want to play if you're not playing

So anyway

Oh yeah

This kid Will also wanted to know if I'd talked to Ethan, but I haven't

None of us have

Ethan answered one text but that was it

I kind of wonder how he's doing though

Must be like

Must be really weird for him right now

I mean it's weird for all of us, but probably especially for him, because of what happened and everything

Wishing it never did, you know?

But

Someone said Ethan deleted all his accounts

I guess he just doesn't want to deal with all this right now

I feel bad for him

I feel like this whole thing started when I hit him

I should have helped him up

If I did, maybe things would've been different

But you can't think like that, right?

But this sucks so bad

Oh, hey, yeah, I also heard the varsity wants to dedicate the season to you

And they want you to come to a game and, like, do the coin toss or something

That would be cool

So, um I should go I guess

Tonight there's this thing at the school

Think about the coin toss thing, okay, Teddy?

Everyone's praying for you

I'll be back tomorrow if it's okay

Hang in there

See you later, Teddy

I'll

Yeah.

## NURSE RICKY

You know what the thing is with growing boys?

You start to stink

That's right

B.O.

And plenty of it

So how about a wash?

How about that bath?

You won't even know I'm here

Well, maybe you will, a little. Just need to shift you around a little bit

That's it

Dang, you're a big kid, you know that?

Good thing I work out

Free weights

But football, I mean come on

Never in a million years my friend

That's a dangerous game

Too dangerous for my blood

Makes people crazy

We were savages once

Still are, I guess, right?

So yeah, no

Not a fan of that crazy game

Whoops

I need to watch my mouth

Now

There we go

Perfect

All good

All perfect on the outside

Now let's get that inside figured out.

Saturday at 2:08 pm

**Rafael** I just wanted to say I don't really know Teddy but one time in the library I couldn't reach a book because I'm short and Teddy was there and he got it down for me and he seemed like a really nice kid so I really really hope he gets better and is okay.

 11

Like · Reply

Saturday at 2:16 pm

**Clea** Yeah I heard he's like the nicest kid ever. Also my friend heard some kids downtown saying that there was a fight during the game or something and that's how Teddy got hurt, does anyone know anything about that??

 3

Like · Reply

Saturday at 2:43 pm

**James** Hey first of all there was no fight, and second of all who are you? it's not cool to spread rumors which you know are BS

 7

Like · Reply

**Camille** Hi Clea are you new? What grade are u in? I don't think I know you but nice to meet you, I agree with james tho, rumors don't help anybody right now, especially Teddy, thanks and I hope to meet you soon at school or wherever!

 18

Like · Reply

## NANA

My, Edward, look at you

You are making me worry you know

You are making me very upset

I'm not happy with you right now, young man

Not happy at all

Your father told me to be nice and upbeat, keep it light

Yes sure

But for me, this is how I do it

By acting normal, right?

Not sugarcoating it

So that's what I'm doing

I'm behaving the way any person would when they see their
grandson lying in a hospital bed

I mean, oh my goodness, look at you

And what did I say about football?

What did I say?

I don't get it

It's a stupid game

Smashing into one another for fun

It's not normal

A young boy like you

Not right

I told your father I didn't want you playing that game

All the newspapers tell you how dangerous it is

I read all the articles and saw the television shows

Grown men, famous football superstars, retired

Now they can't go to the bathroom by themselves

They don't know where they are or who they are

Can't remember their own names

All because of football

Their brains are like scrambled eggs

Everyone knows it

We've all seen it on the news

And what happens?

What happens?

No one listens

Your mother agrees with me, but then she decides to go live her own life, well good for her

Your parents are too busy fighting

No one's paying attention while you go out there and run around like a maniac trying to kill people

You think that makes you a man?

That's not what a man is, Teddy

It's nonsense

I told your father sports make people crazy

They make him crazy

Screaming like an idiot

Win win all the time

The stress and pressure on children

This is the end for you and football

This is it

Such nonsense

Okay, that's enough of that

When you get better we are going to the movies

Popcorn and Raisinets mixed together like always

Right, Teddy?

Right?

Okay, I'm getting it together

If you can stay strong, I can stay strong, am I right?

Am I right, Edward?

Wait a second it's

I think your mother is here

I don't want to see her right now

I just can't

Oh

Your dad is with her

Oh boy

I'm going to go

I don't want to see them together right now

I would get very upset

I don't need that and neither do you, my sweet little boy

Not so little anymore

So I'm going to go

I'm staying at the house

Be back tomorrow

You look as handsome as ever

Such a sweet boy

My sweet little Teddy Bear.

Saturday at 3:07 pm

**Jackson** Teddy I'm pulling for you buddy. You're definitely the most awesome kid and an amazing athlete, probably the best in our grade. I'm proud to be your teammate and I can't wait until you're back on the field with us. I will be there 2night. LET'S GO

 23

Like · Reply

Saturday at 3:26 pm

**Ellie** I heard it wasn't a fight exactly, whoever said that, but something weird definitely happened at the freshmen game, that's how Teddy got hurt. Girls were talking about it at practice

 2

Like · Reply

Saturday at 3:55 pm

**Will** Can we let Teddy get better without all the stuff about was there a fight or not, that's crap and you know it, show some respect everybody

 25

Like · Reply

Saturday at 4:07 pm

**Henry** Hey Will just because you're the captain of the football team doesn't mean you get to bully people . . . we have a right to know the truth. Seriously we all want Teddy to get better but if something else happened, people have a right to know and he would want us to know.

 6

Like · Reply

## DAD

Hey

So, was it good to see Nana?

She's

She's a tough lady, your grandmother

Believe me, I know how tough she is

Teddy, hey guess what

I got a message from Coach Bizetti, he's on his way

He seems like a class act

He said the whole football community is very shaken up

The high school team canceled the first scrimmage

Not surprising, right?

So also, I know they're taking care of this

Getting to the bottom of what happened

All the equipment is going to be reexamined and double-checked

Especially the helmets

The coach is on top of it, and the school too

Which reminds me

I got a call from the principal

I think her name was Dr. Calder?

She's getting involved

She was talking about how this is happening more and more

They're doing studies

They're getting better equipment and medical procedures but there's always a risk

The principal is very concerned

She made it sound like they might drop football or something

So I told her the story about the time you scored three touchdowns last year and afterward I told you we could go out to eat anywhere you wanted to celebrate, and you said you just wanted to eat hot dogs at home with the guys from the team, because you all wanted to be together, and that's what football is all about

I told her you loved the game and we don't blame anyone for what happened

But I think she's worried we're going to sue or something

Everybody is worried about lawsuits these days

But we would never do that of course

Okay, enough about that, let's talk about something else

So guess what?

Janey had her first soccer game today

Mom and I both went

I know, right?

When's the last time that happened?

We were all a little nervous, but Janey played great

They had her at midfield and she got a goal and two assists

It was just a practice game, but you would have gone nuts,

Teddy, I swear

Oh

Hold on, my phone

Someone's calling me, I'll be right back

Hey, Teddy, I'm back, buddy

That was Coach Bizetti

So get this

This is crazy

Believe it or not, he's being told he shouldn't come visit you

I guess there are some people blaming him

Like it's his fault

He told me he had to call a lawyer

A lawyer, can you believe that?

I told him that's ridiculous, he can't control everything that happens on the field

It was an accident

A sports injury

Horrible luck

I told him not to listen to those people who are stirring up trouble

Told him we want him here and that it would be good for you

So he's coming

He's in the middle of organizing this event for tonight, but he's still coming

He seems like someone who really cares about the kids

I swear sometimes I just don't get it, how people can be so hateful

He wants to see you and tell—

Huh?

What?

Whoa, Teddy, did you just squeeze my hand?

I felt that

I'm

I'm going to go find someone okay?

Hey, kiddo, this is great

I'm with you all the way on this thing, Teddy

I'm with you all the way.

**MOM**

Teddy

Teddy

Hi, sweetheart

I just talked to Dad

He told me

He told me you squeezed his hand, Teddy

I can't believe it

I told the nurse, he was so excited

He's getting the doctor

Can you give me a little squeeze?

A little squeeze?

Just a little squeeze, honey?

A little squeeze?

Okay

Whenever you're ready

It can be later

For now, I just want you to rest

Your dad told me he invited Mr. Bizetti to come today

Coach Bizetti

I know he wants to see you

I understand, I'm sure he cares, but I just don't know if this is the right time

I don't even know this man

I understand why your dad thinks he can make these decisions without me—I get it, I really do

But I don't know

I don't know if seeing this man, and being reminded of what happened, is good for you right now

But your father has

Well, you know

So I agreed

And the rest we can discuss later

Because I know you're hearing every word we say to you

I know you're with us

And I really just want you to rest, I really do

So I said okay, but just for a few minutes

And he's bringing his daughter

I don't know her, but Dad says she wants to see you too

And Dr. Sparks says visitors are good

It's good to talk to people

And to listen to people

As long as it's not too much for you

I'm worried it might be getting to be too much

Everyone wants to see you

Everyone loves you

I love you

The nurse, Nurse Ricky, needs to do something now

Hold on, honey

He's going to make you more comfortable okay?

Okay, honey?


**NURSE RICKY**

Careful now . . .

Let me just slide this under your backside . . .

We don't want you staying in one position for too long

The human body needs to move

*You gotta move it move it*

There we go

There

There we go

Oh P.S.

There's a fine young lady outside

Waiting to see you

Bring your A game, son.

Saturday at 4:22 pm

**Amanda** Noooooo I can't believe this is happening right now. I can't believe a sport where people smash their heads against each other is still legal, what is wrong with this country??

 8

Like · Reply

Saturday at 4:29 pm

**Jessica** Uh you're wrong, football is an amazing game and yes injuries are terrible but I'm a girl and I watch it all the time because it is amazing to watch. Baseball is boring, you have to wait forever for something to happen, they just spit and scratch themselves the whole time. Football is total action. And also they are being incredibly careful with safety these days but nothing is 100 percent foolproof. You could get injured in other sports too you know, like people get hurt in soccer and basketball all the time.

16

Like · Reply

Saturday at 4:36 pm

**Emily** Camille wants everyone to go to the thing at the school tonight if possible. Do it for Teddy. I just saw Teddy two days ago at the beach. I am praying for you Teddy with every bone in my body. You are the most awesome guy, so funny and always a smile for everyone. I am crying right now.

15

Like · Reply

## CAMILLE

Hey

Um

Hey, Teddy

It's

Uh

It's really good to see you

I'm so glad I could come

So yeah, um, my dad brought me

We're heading to the high school later

There's going to be a tribute in your honor, Teddy

My dad is outside talking to your parents

They said I could come in

The nurse said it was okay

I didn't know nurses were allowed to wear sunglasses, that's pretty funny

Anyway, I hope it's okay that I came?

It's good to see you

I know you're going to be okay

I know it

I started a page online

And most people are being so nice

But also a few people are writing weird stuff about what happened

Some girl named Clea is like starting rumors and stuff

Like maybe there was a fight or something, and that's how you got hurt

And it makes me so mad

As if my dad would ever let something like that happen

It's like people are looking to blame someone

Or blame football

I know it's violent and stuff, but so are a lot of other sports, and no one is talking about how horrible they are

Anyway, Teddy

So someone said I should take the page down

But I don't know

People need to talk about it

Anyway, what else

I can't believe the summer's almost over, that totally stinks

It was so fun

It was fun, right?

A little weird

The beach was really fun, but I know people were telling you stuff, but I didn't ask them to

Like, I hope you didn't feel pressure to like me back or anything

I never wanted that to happen and I can't believe Emily ever said anything to you

I got so mad at her, we didn't even talk to each other for a few days, we got into this really huge fight, but last night I saw her and we hugged and we cried and we just prayed for you to get better

And also

It's not like I like you because you're popular, I swear

Or the best athlete or anything

I just think you're really nice and funny

And you don't act like a jerk like some kids

I don't mean to be talking about stupid stuff

But I never got a chance to tell you that I hope it didn't make you feel weird, because that was the last thing I wanted

I just want to tell you that I really, really want to talk to you again

Or you to talk to me

I really want you to get better

I really do, okay?

So

Um, yeah, so I'm gonna go get my dad

## COACH

Hello, son

Hello

You look terrific

Just fine

You would never know anything is

You're going to beat this

You're going to whip this thing

You're going to come out of this a stronger person, a better person

You are a tough son of a gun

You are going to take this thing down

You're an athlete

A competitor

And, son

Ted

I want you to know that this is on me

What happened here is on me

I'm responsible for all the kids at preseason camp

You're all my kids, especially you youngsters

Some people don't want me to say that out loud

Some people are telling me to be careful and warning me not to say anything that could get me in trouble, but I say what's in my heart

That's how I've always been

So, yes

We're planning an event for tonight

The community wants to come together and pray for your recovery

The last thing we need to do right now is worry about any of that other stuff

The people who want to shut the program down and run me out of town, all that kind of stuff

Well, the heck with them

They don't know what we're about

They don't know that you kids are like my own kids

You're my family

Everything that happens on my watch is my responsibility

We will get to the bottom of everything

And things will change, son

It's all about keeping my players safe

I promise you that

If things need to change, they will change

Okay then, you take care

I know a few of the other boys are planning on coming by, to check up on you, say hello

The whole team wants to come by, that's right, the whole dang varsity team, but I talked to your folks and we agreed that's a bit much, we don't want the entire hospital to be overrun by football players, now do we, son?

But a few of the boys are going to stop by

These boys are your family

I mean that, son

We're all your family

We're all here for you

I

I did talk to a few of the boys' parents last night

A few of the boys are having a bit of a rough time

That's natural of course

But they're all great kids

We've got counselors talking to them, helping everyone through this

But we all know you're going to be just fine

You've got a terrific family and it's going to be okay

Well then, I should probably head on

Got to get back to it

Planning the event tonight

And of course we're getting ready for the year ahead

Long season

We can't wait to see you up at the high school real soon

We want you with our team, son

In whatever capacity you see fit

It will do us all a world of good

We need you to help us win.

5:19 PM

ALEC

HEY ETHAN JUST CHECKING IN

DID YOU TALK TO ONE OF THOSE
COUNSELORS THIS MORNING?

JUST WANTED TO KNOW HOW IT WENT

I DIDN'T REALLY SAY TOO MUCH

JUST THAT I WAS STILL BASICALLY IN SHOCK

WHICH I AM

LET ME KNOW HOW IT WENT
WHEN YOU HAVE A CHANCE K?

I'M HEADING TO THE THING
AT THE HIGH SCHOOL

IF YOU'RE GOING I'LL SEE YOU THERE

LATER

## JANEY

Ew!

Teddy, it's gross out there

Like a boys' locker room all of a sudden

There are boys outside in the waiting room

Football players I guess

But it's weird

They seem, um, like really nervous and quiet

No one is saying anything

I met this kid Will

Mom and Dad were talking to him

He wants to talk to you

Camille says he's captain of varsity

Hey, guess what?

Tomorrow night, Mom is coming to the house and making fried chicken

Remember when she used to make it and I would get so mad at you?

Remember how you would steal my wings, which were my favorite piece, and I would kick you under the table and you would scream out in pain like I'd actually hurt you? And Mom would yell at me while you were laughing?

And then you would grab another piece of chicken off my plate when Mom and Dad weren't looking and just rip the skin off with your teeth, and sometimes you would even spit it at me, which was so totally disgusting

Remember?

And Mom would end up getting so mad she'd say she would never make fried chicken again, but then she decided that she would because we all liked it so much, and then one time when she made it, I stole the skin from your piece?

And you tickled me until I couldn't breathe and I kicked you under the table again and you pretended to be hurt but Dad realized you weren't really hurt at all and you finally got in trouble that time?

Remember that?

That was so funny

So anyway, I might save you a piece of fried chicken for when you come home

If you're lucky.

**INSIDE**

*Practice*

*Practice*

*Working out*

*Getting stronger*

*Gotta be stronger*

*Make it mean something*

*Make it mean more than anything in the world*

*These are your brothers*

*Your fellow warriors*

*I've waited all my life for this*

*Wildcat Stadium*

*Under the lights*

*People cheering*

*Making my dad proud*

*This is what it's all about*

## MOM

Are you tired, honey?

Are you exhausted?

You've had a lot of action already today

A lot of visitors

People just want to be here

This young man named Will just got here with his parents and some other boys

I'm still concerned it's too much for you

But the doctor said it's okay as long as it's one visitor at a time, just for a few minutes

This might be it for today

I told Will he could come in

The only one

He seems like a good kid

So big and mature, almost like a man

I guess that's why he's the captain

He's only three years older than you, it's almost hard to believe

Scary in a way

The fact that you could be playing football with boys his size is just bizarre

It truly makes no sense, like everything else about this sport

But it is what it is and here we are

Anyway, Will seems like a very nice young man

His mother said he didn't sleep much last night

All the kids seem very sweet

Shy and a little scared

Of course they're scared

It's hard for kids to see other kids suffering

You'll be so happy to see your friends again

When you wake up and see your friends again

You will all be so happy.

## WILL

Dude

Uh

So

Hey, Teddy

Teddy uh

Hey you look like, totally normal

Basically normal

That's awesome

You look great, seriously

Anyway, um

Just wanted to come by and check in

On behalf of the whole team, I just wanted to let you know how bad we're all pulling for you

We're all on your side, man, and uh, I know you're going to be totally fine, because you're a super tough dude

And also, I wanted to let you know, you know, that everything we told you during camp

It was all true

I really hope you can play football again, dude

You're going to be a fantastic football player

You're the best freshman, no doubt

You're already really good, and you work hard and you're super tough

I can tell you want it

I hope you still want to play and you're allowed to play

That would uh

That would suck if you can't

You would've definitely been starting tailback on JV this year

And you'll make varsity next year

Get some playing time

Special teams, punt return, third down situations

I mean, like

You'll be such a good player when you come back for sure

So yeah, I hope you play again

Also

So, hey

Uh, so, that kid Ethan

Can I just

Teddy, if you can hear me

This kid, Ethan, I don't really know him

I didn't really get to know too many of the freshmen kids at camp

But I hope he's cool

I don't

I mean I don't know the kid

But I heard he's kind of messed up about everything

I mean, yeah, of course I get it

He was, you know, he was—

Anyway, the whole thing is messed up

I went to Ethan's house today to see if he was okay

I only saw him for a minute

He didn't want to talk to me, or even see me, to be honest

I feel bad for him

But, uh, you know

I didn't get mad at him or anything

I just asked him if he was going to say anything about what
happened

And, you know, about the Hit Parade and the prizes and stuff

And he said no, he swears no

So that's cool

I just

I'm not sure if you can hear me, dude

I just really, really want you to get better

I mean like I remember playing in the Rookie Rumble when I was a freshman

I thought it was the coolest thing in the world, you know?

Nothing like this has ever happened before

That's why everyone is so freaked out

We need you to get better

No one has to

No one has to—

Oh hey, Mrs. Youngblood.



## MOM

I think Teddy needs to rest, okay, Will?

You can come back another time

Maybe tomorrow

I know Teddy is so pleased that you and the other boys care so much

Your support really means so much to all of us, it really does

But I think, for now, Teddy just needs to rest.

**WILL**

Oh absolutely, Mrs. Youngblood

Absolutely

I just wanted to

I wanted Teddy to know the whole varsity was pulling for him

Is pulling for him

We are uh

Okay

Thanks, Mrs. Youngblood

See ya, Ted.


**ALEC**

Hey

I'm heading to the high school soon for the event thing, but your parents said it was cool if I said hey for a minute first

So, um

I talked to Will outside for a second, and he told me he talked to Ethan

He's not

Ethan's not really talking to anyone right now

But uh, nobody wants you to worry about anything

Everyone just wants you to get better

Ethan still isn't answering texts

I guess I'll talk to him when school starts

I'm pretty sure he doesn't want to make this into a thing

He just wants it to go away, but it's hard, you know?

It's hard not to talk about it

Like I mean I kind of want to tell somebody what happened
because I think it might help

But uh, I won't

I promise I won't.

# WALTHORNENEWS.COM

SATURDAY, AUGUST 27 10:07 PM

## Young Athlete Injured; Town Gathers to Offer Hope

A townwide vigil was held at Walthorne High School tonight to pray for the recovery of Edward Youngblood, 13, who was seriously injured Friday at preseason football camp. Edward, who is scheduled to begin his freshman year at Walthorne High next week, is currently at TriCounty Memorial Hospital with unspecified injuries.

"He's a terrific kid," said Louis Bizetti, Walthorne's head football coach, who has also been a physical education instructor at the school for sixteen years. "It's just so awful when something like this happens, and it's important that the community come together to show our support and concern for Teddy and his family. We love our football in this town, but we love our football players even more."

The Wildcats, who finished with a record of 8–2 last year, return with a solid roster of varsity athletes and are expected to contend for the state crown this year.

There has been no word on whether or not the season will begin as scheduled.

Saturday at 10:19 pm

**Camille** It was so great to see everyone there tonight at the celebration for Teddy, thank you all for coming, it was incredible and meant so much to Teddy's family.

👍 25

Like · Reply

Saturday at 10:26 pm

**Becky** It was beautiful, it really was, your dad made an amazing speech Camille, you should be so proud of him

👍 16

Like · Reply

Saturday at 10:29 pm

**Camille** I am
I love my dad 😊

👍 18

Like · Reply

Saturday at 10:37 pm

**Stephanie** It was a really nice event but what was up at the end, why did it end so suddenly like that?

Like · Reply

Saturday at 10:49 pm

**Rebecca** The vigil was so beautiful. Everyone is in total shock right now, we are all praying for Teddy. You're right tho it did end a little weird, I think maybe from what I heard there was like a little argument because some people were asking questions, and then other people were talking about maybe somebody is hiding something about what really happened when Teddy got hurt. I saw your dad get mad at some people Camille and he was absolutely right that wasn't the place for people to be spreading rumors.

 8

Like · Reply

Saturday at 10:51 pm

**Clea** I agree, it was a beautiful ceremony but it did feel like something was up at the end. If something else happened to Teddy, like other than just a normal football thing, then I hope somebody says something

Like · Reply

Saturday at 11:07 pm

**Janey** Hi everyone. Teddy is my brother and I want to thank everyone for coming tonight and for their good wishes. It really means a lot to my family but can those of you guys who are talking about the other stuff and spreading rumors please stop. We just want Teddy to get better. Thank you all very much.

 30

Like · Reply

Saturday at 11:20 pm

**Camille** Thank you Janey! You are so brave!!! And I completely agree!!

 17

Like · Reply

GUYS

I WENT TO SEE TEDDY TODAY

I SERIOUSLY FREAKIN ALMOST CRIED
SEEING THAT KID LYING THERE

HE IS SO TOUGH

IT MADE ME PROUD TO BE A WALTHORNE WILDCAT

BECAUSE THAT'S WHO WE ARE

WE'RE TOUGH

WE'RE PROUD

WE'RE A TEAM

EVERYONE NEEDS TO PRAY FOR HIS
RECOVERY AND REMEMBER TO BE COOL

PEOPLE ARE STARTING TO
SPREAD RUMORS AND STUFF

SO IT'S MORE IMPORTANT THAN
EVER TO STICK TOGETHER

OTHERWISE WE COULD LOSE EVERYTHING

THE TEAM, THE SEASON, OUR CHANCE AT STATES

EVERYTHING

IT WILL ALL BE OVER
EVERYONE PLEASE REMEMBER THAT

SUNDAY, AUGUST 28
8:30 AM

**PATIENT REPORT**

BRAIN SWELLING REDUCED.
CONTINUE TO MONITOR FOR INTERNAL
BLEEDING.
POSSIBLE RESPONSE TO VERBAL
COMMUNICATION.
POSSIBLE RESPONSE TO HAND SQUEEZE.
RAPID EYE MOVEMENT WITH LIDS REMAINING
CLOSED.
HOURLY MONITORING OF ALL VITAL SIGNS AND
EVIDENCE OF COMMUNICATION.

**CONDITION: CRITICAL**

HEY ETHAN

WERE YOU THERE LAST NIGHT?

I DIDN'T SEE YOU

LISTEN DUDE SORRY TO KEEP TEXTING YOU BUT IF YOU FEEL LIKE YOU NEED TO TALK TO SOMEONE JUST LET ME KNOW

AND YO I KNOW I MESSED UP TOO

I TOTALLY SHOULD HAVE HELPED YOU UP AFTER THAT HIT

THIS IS NOT ALL ON YOU

I HOPE YOU KNOW THAT

Sunday at 9:44 am

**Amy** I was at the vigil and I agree it was so nice but I could tell there was some rumor going around or something. The thing about a fight though is weird, I thought Teddy got hurt playing football, like a concussion but worse?

 5

Like · Reply

Sunday at 9:57 am

**Nick** I was there when Teddy got hurt, I'm on the high school football team. there was no fight it was just football stuff, if you don't know what you're talking about you should step off, seriously.

18

Like · Reply

Sunday at 10:04 am

**Joey** I'm on the football team too, you kids who haven't even started high school yet shouldn't be on sites like this so stop spreading BS rumors and grow up.

 8

Like · Reply

Sunday at 10:12 am

**Emily** This is supposed to be a page to pray for Teddy's recovery please stop arguing with each other that's so not cool.

👍 20

Like · Reply

Sunday at 11:16 am

**Clea** I heard the police were there.

Like · Reply

MR. RASHAD: Nice to see you again, Ethan.

ETHAN: You too.

MR. RASHAD: Everything okay? You want some water or juice?

ETHAN: No, I'm good, thanks.

MR. RASHAD: Great. So, did you go to the vigil last night?

ETHAN: No, I, uh, couldn't make it.

MR. RASHAD: Ah. Well, I heard it was a really nice event. When something like this happens, sometimes it helps to be with other people who are going through the same thing, to all come together and support each other.

ETHAN: Yeah.

MR. RASHAD: But not for you, huh?

ETHAN:          I was really tired.

MR. RASHAD:     I'll bet. How about today? Did you
                sleep okay last night?

ETHAN:          Not great, but uh, okay I guess.

MR. RASHAD:     Well, I'd really like to help you
                deal with this whole thing, and the
                first step is making sure you fully
                comprehend exactly what happened to
                your friend. It seems there still
                might be some confusion about that.

ETHAN:          What do you mean?

MR. RASHAD:     Well, there are a few conflicting
                reports about what did exactly
                happen, which is not at all uncommon
                in situations like this. Everyone's
                memories are different, especially
                when something traumatic occurs.

ETHAN:          Conflicting reports from who?

MR. RASHAD:     I really just want to concentrate on
                what you remember and how it made you
                feel.

ETHAN:          Well, I know what I saw. It's like I
                said before, we were playing in the
                Rookie Rumble, and something must
                have happened to Teddy, he took a
                hit I guess, but no one noticed and
                he didn't tell anyone. Then after
                practice was over and we were hanging
                around, he fell. Like, just collapsed,
                from one second to the next.

MR. RASHAD:     How did you react? Did you try to help
                him?

ETHAN:          Of course. I mean, we all did. The
                coaches came right away. Someone
                called 911 and then they told us to
                leave the field.

MR. RASHAD:     That must have been so hard for you,
                to leave your friend.

ETHAN:          It was horrible.

MR. RASHAD:     You mentioned he took a hit. Was it a
                particularly hard hit?

ETHAN:          I guess. I mean, I don't really
                remember. It was the Rookie Rumble, so
                everyone was hitting hard.

MR. RASHAD:   What do you mean exactly? What does
              the Rookie Rumble have to do with it?

ETHAN:        It's like this big tradition, where
              every year, on the last day of camp,
              the seniors coach the incoming
              freshmen in a scrimmage, and it's a
              big deal, because we're all trying to
              prove ourselves to the older kids. So
              everyone was playing really hard.

MR. RASHAD:   Aha, so kids are coaching other kids?
              Where are the regular coaches?

ETHAN:        I think some were on the hill watching
              and taking notes, a few others were
              training the sophomores and juniors,
              stuff like that.

MR. RASHAD:   Sounds like quite an opportunity to
              prove yourself. How did you feel? Were
              you excited? Nervous?

ETHAN:        I guess. It's really competitive. Like
              I said, everyone tries to impress the
              seniors so they'll tell the coaches
              how tough we are. It's the first time
              they've ever seen any of us play in a
              game.

MR. RASHAD:   What position did you play? Did you
              feel like you played well?

ETHAN:        I thought I did pretty good. I mean,
              I'm small, but I'm pretty quick, so
              they put me at outside linebacker.
              I got hit really hard once or twice,
              this kid Alec hit me really hard on
              one play, but I made some tackles.

MR. RASHAD:   So it was full pads, full hitting,
              everything?

ETHAN:        Yeah, full pads and stuff. Also it
              was really hot. I think maybe Teddy
              collapsed because of that.

MR. RASHAD:   Well, sure, yes, that may have had
              something to do with it. But his
              brain was injured. Bleeding. His head
              must have taken a real wallop at some
              point.

ETHAN:        I guess, yeah. But anyway, how many
              more days do we have to talk about
              this? I don't get it. Kids get hurt
              all the time.

MR. RASHAD:   Not quite like this, Ethan. But these

conversations are certainly something you don't have to do if you don't want to. That's up to you and your parents.

ETHAN: Well, I mean, of course it's a really horrible thing that happened. But this is like, this feels like it's making it worse.

MR. RASHAD: I get why you feel that way.

ETHAN: Then can we stop? I just want to go home and not think about it. I want to be left alone.

MR. RASHAD: Well, that's just it, Ethan—I'm not sure it's a great idea for you to be alone at a time like this. I think it's better to be with people, to talk about it. And I think your parents agree with me.

ETHAN: Okay fine, whatever.

MR. RASHAD: Did you enjoy being at camp with the older kids?

ETHAN: I guess.

MR. RASHAD:    Were they cool? Friendly? Didn't give
               you young guys too much of a hard time
               or anything?

ETHAN:         What? What does that have to do with
               anything?

MR. RASHAD:    I'm just curious how it made you feel,
               that's all.

ETHAN:         Can I go?

MR. RASHAD:    Sure, you can.

ETHAN:         I need to go.

**INSIDE**

*Keep working*

*Keep working*

*In the heat*

*In the rain*

*Early in the morning*

*Late at night*

*There is nothing better than being on the team*

*You will never work harder*

*You will never feel closer*

*You will never be prouder*

*This is what life is*

*Life is football*

*Football is life*

*Down*

*Up*

*Down*

*Up*

*Be the best*

*I can do this*

*I can get bigger*

*I can get faster*

*I can get stronger*

*I can get meaner*

*Listen to the coaches*

*Listen to the captains*

*Follow them*

*Do what they say*

*Do what they do*

*I can do this*

*I can do this*

*Practice*

*Practice*

*Practice*

*Sweat*

*Be a man*

*Be men*

*Prove it*

*Do it*

*Do it*

*Do it for the team*

*Be men*

*There is nothing better*

*There is nothing better*

*There is nothing*

## MOM

Good morning, sweetie

I

I didn't sleep much last night

I was up thinking

And I decided that, well, I wanted to talk to you about something

Something I haven't really been able to talk about with anyone

Something you deserve to know

So

So here goes

The day I left

I wasn't planning on leaving

It was supposed to be a day like any other day. You were already out the door, I was getting your sister ready for school, we had a few minutes before the bus was supposed to come, I was making her lunch, and I just started to cry. I was frozen, I couldn't move. I had no idea what was going on, that had never happened before, but there I was, crying, and Janey walked in and asked me what was wrong, and I couldn't tell her, because I wasn't sure I knew myself. Or maybe I just couldn't admit it to myself, or anyone else. I couldn't tell her that I was unhappy, that Daddy and I weren't sure we still loved each other, that I missed having time to paint, and that I loved you both too much to let you see your mom falling apart. So instead, I just told her I heard something sad on TV, and later that morning, I was staring into the mirror, and I realized that the only thing I could do to save myself and save my relationship with the two of you was to leave and to figure out a way to live so that I could be what the two of you needed me to be

And I know I've told you and Janey this over and over, but I'm not sure you've ever believed me, so I just want to say again that this was never about not loving you guys or not wanting to be your mom

If anything it was about loving you too much

And figuring out a way to make myself a better person and a better mom

The mom that you both deserve

And I will always be there for you

Always always

So that's what I wanted to say

Oh

Here, let me fix that

I've told the nurses ten times not to let your pillow get scrunched up

I told them how you like it kind of folded under your head

So, Teddy

Last night there was a vigil at the high school

It was very moving

You would have hated all the attention though

But I wanted to tell you

I don't want you to worry but there was something

There were some people who were talking

They might have been parents, I couldn't be sure

But they were saying that they'd heard stuff about what
happened to you

Like there was more to the story, and people were hiding
something

I guess it's standard when something like this happens

But other parents weren't happy about it and told them to be
quiet

The coach was not happy at all

He asked them to stop disturbing the event

Other people told them it was inappropriate to talk that way at
a ceremony of hope and community and recovery, but I'm not
sure I agree

I think we should get to the bottom of it

I'm not looking to blame someone, this isn't just me hating
football or anything like that, I promise

I just want answers

Like, for instance, why are freshmen practicing with seniors on
ninety-degree days?

I don't get that

Your father disagrees, of course

He thinks this Coach Bizetti is a god

We talked about it last night

The same argument about football we always used to have

Dad was very stubborn

He said you don't really practice with the older boys, just do stretches with them

And the younger kids love it because they worship the upperclassmen

Whatever, it just seems wrong

Believe it or not, your dad even thinks you might play again someday, which is pretty much the craziest thing I've ever heard

On this, Nana and I agree at least

I think he's in denial because of the shock, but still it's crazy

This whole sport is crazy

Oh sure, everybody says the same thing, football is dangerous, sometimes players get hurt, I'm not sure what the parents can do to stop that

That's what they say

But guess what?

I think there's a lot that parents can do actually

Parents need to do the research

They need to know the risks

They need to be more aware than I was, that's for sure

Way more aware than I was

I have no one to blame but myself

Honey!

Did you just

Did you just move your eyebrows?

Am I upsetting you?

Oh no, I shouldn't be talking about this

Are you okay?

I saw something

Oh my gosh

I should get the doctor

Hold on

Let me get her




I just told Nurse Ricky

He said it's just something that happens

But the doctor will be here later of course

Ricky is great

Everyone is so concerned

Alec is waiting outside, he just got here

He still seems so upset

He is taking this really hard

Daddy is picking up Nana and I have to take Janey to practice, so Alec will keep you company for a little while

I know today is going to be a good day for you

We are all ready for a good day

Sweetie

We're all ready for a good day, aren't we?

## ALEC

Yo, Teddy

It's just me this time

Your mom just left

Your dad's not here yet

My parents said I could come say hey

I told them I haven't been sleeping that great and it makes me feel a little better to come by, so they said okay

I just yeah

You know I think maybe

I wanted to tell you

I think maybe people are starting to wonder about how you really got hurt

This therapist lady I've been talking to was all about how I was doing at first, but now she's asking me a lot of questions about what happened, almost like she's a cop or something

I mean I haven't told her anything

But it's hard, Teddy

It's hard not talking about it

I feel like bursting sometimes

And I get being loyal to the team and everything, but it doesn't feel right

And last night at the ceremony thing, people were asking questions like they know something

It's like, it's gonna come out at some point you know?

Hey

I can see your eyes moving beneath your eyelids

That's so

Is that good?

Is that a good thing?

It's

Wow

They're darting back and forth

Teddy?

I'm getting

Hold on, I'm getting somebody.


## INSIDE

*Don't be lazy*

*Don't be late*

*Don't miss practice unless you're dead or dying*

*Don't talk back*

*Don't question the coaches*

*And most important*

*Don't be soft*

*Do not be soft you hear me?*

*DO NOT BE SOFT*


## NURSE RICKY

Easy

Easy, fella

You're sweating

You're drenched

You're having some sort of something

A dream

A bad dream

Okay now

Let me take care of this

We got you

We got you.

## DR. SPARKS

Hello, young man

It's good to see you

I understand you've been doing some serious thinking

Dreaming

Worrying, even

Well, we don't want you worrying about anything

We're taking good care of you

But we need you to take care of you too

We need to be careful

We want you relaxed and resting

You need rest, Mr. Youngblood

Rest, relax, recovery

We're going to help you relax so you don't have to worry about anything

You just take it easy, okay?

Sunday at 2:14 pm

**Liam** I agree with Nick and James and those guys, people need to stop dumping on football and football players, it's like you're jealous or something, you guys gotta knock it off. Teddy's a great kid and he's going to be a stud football player some day, you watch.

👍 15

Like · Reply

Sunday at 2:37 pm

**Adam** I saw Mr. Rashad downtown at the library talking to Ethan.

Like · Reply

Sunday at 3:11 pm

**Rebecca** Who's Mr. Rashad? What were they doing?

Like · Reply

Sunday at 3:13 pm

**Adam** He's a counselor at school, my older brother knows him. I have no idea but it looked like an intense conversation.

 1

Like · Reply

Sunday at 4:11 pm

**Will** Everyone on the football team needs to chill out and stop acting like idiots or get off this thread right now.

10

Like · Reply

**DAD**

Hey, bud

The doctor told us what's going on

She, uh

She told us about something called unconscious thought

Like dreams

You're not asleep but you're not awake

The doctor said it's a sign of increased brain activity, which is awesome

But she said you seem agitated

And she's concerned about overstimulation

So

First of all, it's our fault for talking about some of this other stuff, so that's not going to happen again

But also she is going to change your medication a little bit to help you rest

Maybe not have so many visitors

All these people want to see you, but Mom and I think it's too much

So for now just close family and friends

Less noise I think will be good

Camille is here, she came with her dad and she has a gift for you

She's going to say a quick hello just for a minute

You just need to rest and get strong

Nothing else matters.

**Hipstuh** Who was at the rally last night for Teddy? Did you see the cops? There were cops there.

Like · Reply

**Nick** It wasn't a rally, it was a vigil. Wow get your terms straight Mr. Hipstuh.

 4

Like · Reply

**Sloane** I don't get it tho, why would cops be there?

Like · Reply

**Clea** Has anyone talked to some kid named Ethan?

Like · Reply

Sunday at 7:19 pm

**Andrea** Ethan who?

Like · Reply

Sunday at 7:28 pm

**Clea** I don't know his last name but somebody said he knows something.

Like · Reply

Sunday at 7:33 pm

**Rebecca** R u talking about Ethan Metzger? I think he disconnected his phone or something, no one has heard from him.

Like · Reply

## CAMILLE

Hey

I don't want to bother you but, um, I brought you a present

It's stupid, but I thought maybe you would think it was funny

I don't know

Remember, like, a couple of weeks ago at the beach, you were playing volleyball with your friends and you saw me walking to the Sandy Grille with Olivia and Emily, and you called out, "Yo Bizetti, bring me back some fries?" And I was going to, I swear I was, but then Olivia said it would be stupid and it would look dumb for me to just like drop everything and do whatever you asked me to, and besides, she said you weren't even serious, you were just showing off for your friends, so she convinced me not to. And then remember when I walked back, you yelled, "Seriously? No fries?" And you and all your friends laughed and I laughed too but then later I felt bad that I didn't get them for you, but Olivia and Emily told me that I was acting like a third grader, which made me feel like an idiot, so for like the next week I barely said anything to you? Remember that?

I feel, like, I felt like so bad about that, and I really did want to bring you those fries, so, uh, I brought them today

That's like the stupidest gift in the world to bring someone in, you know, in your situation, I know, but I just, I just wanted to

So anyway

My dad is talking to your parents in the waiting room

I'm not sure what they're talking about, I think it has something to do with last night

Some of the kids were acting a little weird

At first I thought it was because they were just really upset and freaked out about this whole thing, but then someone said that people were asking questions about what happened

Someone even said the police were there

Which is so weird, right?

So my dad found out and kind of went ballistic

He said everyone who was talking about what happened should leave

He wanted to make sure no one was distracted, because the whole point was for people to pray and think about you and just focus on you getting better

I don't know what's happening, Teddy

People are getting weird online too, people are saying stuff

I don't get it

I feel so bad for my dad

All he's ever done his whole life is care about his players

Ugh, so

I'm going to have a few of the fries, is that okay?

Should I give them to that nurse guy?

He's hilarious by the way

Or maybe your parents will want them?

What I

What I really want is for you to eat them.

Sunday at 8:12 pm

**Emily** I am thinking about Teddy. We should all be thinking about Teddy and what he and his poor family are going through. Please please please stop with this other nonsense and just focus on what's important and that is our friend getting better I beg you guys.

👍 10

Like · Reply

Sunday at 8:56 pm

**Ephraim** I agree! I'm just reading this now for the first time and it's pretty gross. And seriously stop with the conspiracy theories it's not helping at all!!!

👍 12

Like · Reply

Sunday at 9:15 pm

**Clea** I'm not exactly sure what a conspiracy theory is but I've heard from like three people at least that this was not just a football injury, that there is some kind of organized thing on the last day of camp where kids on the team beat each other up for fun, like some sort of competition, it's a tradition or something, has anyone else heard about this?

👍 4

Like · Reply

Sunday at 9:44 pm

**James** Clea whoever you are you need to stop talking RIGHT NOW, you seriously have no idea what you're talking about. 14

Like · Reply

**INSIDE**

*Squirts*

*Punks*

*You ready to be part of Walthorne Wildcat football*

*You think you're ready*

*Time to find out*

*Heat*

*Sweat*

*Drenched*

*Heavy*

*Shouting*

*Crazy*

*Start*

*Hurry up*

*Start*

*Ready*

*Now*

*Do it*

## MOM

Hi, honey

I'm back

Janey and I had fried chicken tonight

I saved you some

Dad's with her at the house, but I'll be here all night sleeping right next to you

I

I don't know what's happening

Today was

Today was a long day

I just

I'll be quiet now

Today was a long day

But I think you're better

You really seem better to me

I just want you to get better

I just want you back, Teddy.

Sunday at 10:02 pm

**Susie** I don't get why everyone is being so mean to each other when one of our classmates is in the hospital like fighting for his life.

 17

Like · Reply

Sunday at 10:19 pm

**Jackson** People are jerks online sometimes, that's why.

 8

Like · Reply

Sunday at 10:48 pm

**Wassup** Why does wanting the truth make people jerks? #TruthIsFreedom

 4

Like · Reply

MONDAY, AUGUST 29

8:00 AM

**PATIENT REPORT**

FURTHER REDUCTION OF BRAIN SWELLING.
BREATHING ON HIS OWN FOR LIMITED PERIODS.
REMAINS FREE OF ANY SIGNS OF INTERNAL
BLEEDING.

**CONDITION: GUARDED**

**INSIDE**

*Hey, Teddy*

*I'm Will*

*I'm one of the captains*

*I've been watching you*

*You can really play*

*You're going to do great things on this team*

*So*

*We want you to be part of something special*

*Come on*

*It'll be fun*

*Makes you part of the program*

*Makes us all brothers*

*It's cool*

*Pretty intense*

*You seem like someone who would be totally into it*

*Are you down?*

*Are you one of us?*

*Cool*

*Very cool*

*It happens during the Rookie Rumble*

*We call it the Hit Parade*

*Here's how it works*

Monday at 8:14 am

**Clea** Something other than football happened for sure. I heard someone came up behind Teddy at the end of practice and decked him or pushed him and he hit his head.

Like · Reply

Monday at 8:23 am

**Nick** Heard where? Why would someone do that? That's the stupidest thing I ever heard, whoever said that is a moron.

 5

Like · Reply

Monday at 9:18 am

**James** This is pathetic.

👍 3

Like · Reply

Monday at 9:22 am

**Will** VARSITY FOOTBALL PLAYERS OFF THIS THREAD
DO NOT POST
I MEAN IT

Like · Reply

MR. RASHAD:   How are you doing today?

ETHAN:        Fine.

MR. RASHAD:   I thought we'd meet here for a little
              change of pace. Can I order you some
              breakfast?

ETHAN:        No thanks, I'm not really hungry.

MR. RASHAD:   Got it. Well, thanks for coming. I hope
              you're okay with the earlier hour. They
              say the brain works at maximum capacity
              an hour after you wake up.

ETHAN:        [INAUDIBLE]

MR. RASHAD:   How did you sleep last night? A little
              better?

ETHAN:        Pretty good.

MR. RASHAD:   That's great. I'm just asking because
              your parents are a little worried.

ETHAN:           You talked to them?

MR. RASHAD:      Of course. I talk to them every day.

ETHAN:           They always worry about stuff.

MR. RASHAD:      That's because they're good parents,
                 and good parents worry.

ETHAN:           So what did they say?

MR. RASHAD:      Well . . . they seem to think you're
                 not sleeping too well.

ETHAN:           I mean, it's not like I didn't see my
                 friend collapse right in front of me.
                 And now he's in a coma and he might
                 die and I'm supposed to just sleep
                 like a baby? Wouldn't that make me
                 like a psychopath or something?

MR. RASHAD:      Your parents know you pretty well,
                 obviously, and they're concerned.

ETHAN:           Meaning what?

MR. RASHAD:      Meaning, they seem to think there may
                 be something else going on.

ETHAN:         That's crazy.

MR. RASHAD:    Well, maybe, but perhaps there's
               something that you don't feel ready to
               talk about. Or almost feel ready to
               talk about.

ETHAN:         Like what?

MR. RASHAD:    You tell me.

ETHAN:         I already told you what happened. You
               can ask anyone who was there.

MR. RASHAD:    Okay.

ETHAN:         I looked it up online. Concussions.
               Head injuries. It happens all the time
               in football.

MR. RASHAD:    You looked it up? Why?

ETHAN:         What do you mean, why? I just—I wanted
               to know more about it.

MR. RASHAD:    Okay.

ETHAN:         So everyone should just leave me alone

and stop acting like there's some big
mystery.

MR. RASHAD:     Okay.

ETHAN:          Can I go? I'm not hungry and I don't
                really have anything to say.

MR. RASHAD:     Of course. Just—just one more thing.

ETHAN:          What?

MR. RASHAD:     Is it true you're quitting football?

ETHAN:          I—Where did you hear that?

MR. RASHAD:     Well, your mom mentioned to me that
                you were supposed to go in for
                your JV uniform fitting yesterday
                afternoon, but you told her you
                didn't want to go.

ETHAN:          That doesn't mean anything.

MR. RASHAD:     I thought you loved football.

ETHAN:          I did. I mean, I do. I just—I haven't
                figured it out yet. I haven't decided.

MR. RASHAD:   Well, I get that. That's
              understandable, after an event like
              this. It's a lot to process.

ETHAN:        I'm gonna go now. I don't think—I
              don't think this is doing anything.

MR. RASHAD:   Okay, Ethan. Good to see you. I'll see
              you tomorrow.

ETHAN:        Tomorrow? Seriously?

MR. RASHAD:   Just for a few minutes. Just a quick
              check-in.

ETHAN:        I don't know what else we have to talk
              about.

MR. RASHAD:   Maybe nothing.

ETHAN:        I don't see why I have to keep doing
              this.

MR. RASHAD:   You don't. No one is forcing you.

ETHAN:        Well my parents keep telling me I have
              to come. But maybe I'll skip it. No
              offense or anything.

MR. RASHAD:     None taken. Maybe I'll see you
                tomorrow, and maybe I won't.

ETHAN:          I just don't want to think about it
                anymore. Talking about it doesn't make
                anything better, it makes it worse.

MR. RASHAD:     I totally understand why you feel that
                way.

ETHAN:          I don't ever want to talk about it
                again for as long as I live.

## DAD

Oh man, what a morning

I could seriously cry right now, seeing you without that tube in your mouth, even for a few minutes

This is it, Teddy, we're on the long road back, the beginning of the end of this whole nightmare

Listen, Ted, I need to tell you something

I haven't told your mom yet

She is dealing with a lot of her own stuff

I'm not sure she's ready to handle this right at this second

But it's totally

I had a visit from the police last night

And they, uh

They asked a few questions

Told me a few things I wasn't

I didn't know about some of it

I was led to believe this was a football injury, nothing more

A head injury

That's what I've been told by everyone

The coach gave me his word

Now suddenly I'm hearing other stuff

I mean uh

Mom has been saying it for years

We all know football's a rough sport

People get hurt, kids get hurt, it's all part of the game

But, son, if something happened

If somebody did something to you on purpose

Well, that's

I can't even begin to

And I understand the team mentality, the need to belong

When I was in college, our fraternity did some crazy things

You pay your dues, you go through some stuff, you act like an idiot and do idiotic stuff sometimes, that's part of the deal, I get all that, I do

But you guys are just kids

Just kids

If somebody did something to you I

Okay

You need to get better first of all

I'm just

I guess I might be losing it a little

I only want you to get better and not worry about any of this

But the police seem to think something else went on

And I just want to make sure you know that if something happened

If someone did something to you, if any of these kids did anything to you, I will make it right

I will protect you with every last breath in my body

I will find out what happened and I will make it right—


**MOM**

Jim

What are you talking about

Make what right?

Our son is in here fighting for his life

Please don't upset him

And look at this pillow

How many times do I have to tell them how he likes his pillow

Why is this so difficult to understand, I've shown them a thousand times

**DAD**

Sarah, can I

Can we talk outside for a minute?

**MOM**

What?

**DAD**

We should talk outside, Sarah.

**MOM**

Fine

Fine

Be right back, Teddy.

Monday at 11:09 am

**Rebecca** So now people are saying it's like this thing the football players do, like sometimes the older kids beat up the younger kids, it's like something you have to do if you want to be on the team.

Like · Reply

Monday at 12:16 pm

**Eric** Yeah right. As if the coaches would allow that.

 3

Like · Reply

Monday at 1:27 pm

**Susie** Nice tribute page you guys. Way to support each other and share thoughts about Teddy. Good going.

 5

Like · Reply

Monday at 2:24 pm

**Britt** Guidance counselors or therapists are talking to all the kids who were there and somebody said now they're trying to figure out what really happened, so like maybe whoever said it wasn't just a football injury was right after all.

Like · Reply

Monday at 2:49 pm

**Clea** I heard that too, that's what I've been saying.

Like · Reply

Monday at 4:39 pm

**Amanda** Shut up you guys, seriously I mean it. Just get off this page if you want to be like that.

Like · Reply

## JANEY

Teddy

I have to be quiet

Mom and Dad didn't even see me come in here just now because they're in the visitors' lounge and they're whispering to each other. They think they're being quiet, but everyone can hear them

Nana is here too

She's talking to this man whose wife is really sick or something. He's really nice even though he's sad. He brings me back a chocolate milk from the cafeteria when he goes down there. He was in the lounge before we came in—I think maybe he could hear what Mom and Dad were saying

They were kind of fighting, Mom and Dad, but not about the usual stuff

Different stuff, like, I think it has to do with last night

It was crazy. I looked out the window and I couldn't believe it, a police car in our driveway, lights flashing, so weird

I freaked out

Ollie was barking his head off. He hates strangers, remember?

This policeman ended up talking with Dad outside the front door for like five minutes, maybe like ten, but Dad was kind of different after that, he was quiet all night, I mean he's been really quiet the last few days obviously but even quieter than usual

Mom was at her apartment, so she doesn't know about the police thing, and Dad told me he doesn't want to tell her yet, he's nervous she'll get like freaked out or something

I think the police think something happened, that somebody did something to you

Did they?

Did, like, someone hurt you on purpose?

I probably shouldn't be in here talking about this, but I just want to know what happened and everyone else wants to know

I went to the beach today and everyone was talking about it

I wish you could tell Mom and Dad

They really need to know—



**MOM**

Janey

You can't be in here right now

We need to let him rest.



**DAD**

Sarah

Sarah, please don't raise your voice, I know you think you're talking at a normal tone of voice, you don't hear it, but the rest of us hear it, please

We cannot bring our stress in here

We're both doing it and we have to stop

I get how frustrating this is

We will address this, we will fix it, but not now

**MOM**

If not now, when?

If not now, then when?

You just told me there are rumors something else may have happened, and you expect me not to react?

Why didn't I know about this?

**DAD**

Well, to be honest, you don't generally want to be kept in the loop on any football stuff

**MOM**

Please don't be unfair

This is different and you know it

I need to know what is happening

Tell me what is happening


**DAD**

Fine, you're right

But I don't know

I'm as confused as you

And please let's not get into this now

Not while our son is lying here

We can discuss it later

Right now, can we just focus on him?

No outside visitors today, none

We just need to be with him, and take care of him, and—

Oh

Oh my God

OH MY GOD.

**INSIDE**

*Color*

*Form*

*Shape*

*Brightness*

*Sound*

*Distant sound*

*Darkness inside the light*

*Circles*

*Memories I almost remember*

*Thoughts*

*Thoughts*

*But no words*

*Still no words*

**DAD**

Janey.

**MOM**

Janey, look.

**DAD**

It's Teddy

It's your brother

Teddy

He opened his eyes

He opened his eyes.

Monday at 9:18 pm

**Camille** I haven't read the page for a while but now looking at all this stuff I'm thinking about taking it down. I wish I never started it. You guys are so gross, I didn't realize people could be so ugly and insensitive.

 19

Like · Reply

Monday at 9:32 pm

**Wassup** Camille do you have a crush on Teddy? Because you are sure acting like u do.

👍 3

Like · Reply

Monday at 10:01 pm

**Rebecca** Can we please not do this? Can we please remember who we are, that we're nice people and one of our friends is in trouble. PLEASE.

👍 14

Like · Reply

Monday at 10:59 pm

**Wassup** As soon as we can all admit the truth, that kids do stupid things sometimes, to themselves and to each other, and covering it up makes it so much worse.

 5

Like · Reply

Monday at 11:08 pm

**Clea** I agree ^^
We need to talk about it
It helps to talk about this stuff.

 4

Like · Reply

ETHAN

I HAVE NO IDEA IF YOU'RE LOOKING AT TEXTS BUT IF YOU ARE

I WANTED TO LET U KNOW THAT PEOPLE ARE STARTING TO FIGURE OUT WHAT HAPPENED

IT'S ONLY A MATTER OF TIME BEFORE EVERYTHING COMES OUT

I HOPE YOU'RE OKAY

TEXT ME BACK OKAY?

PLEASE

I HAVE SOMETHING I HAVE TO TELL YOU

IT'S IMPORTANT

**DAD**

They were open

For a moment

Teddy's eyes were open

I swear

They were open

And clear

And blue

And strong

And

I saw

He was here

He was right here with us

He was back


Our Teddy was back.

# PART TWO

TUESDAY, AUGUST 30

8:08 AM

**PATIENT REPORT**

SEMI-COMATOSE, IMPROVED RESPONSE TO
VERBAL STIMULI.
EYES BRIEFLY OPENED OVERNIGHT.
NON-VERBAL RESPONSIVENESS TO TOUCH.
BRAIN SWELLING FURTHER REDUCED.
BREATHING WITHOUT ASSISTANCE FOR SHORT
PERIODS.

**CONDITION: SERIOUS**

TUESDAY, AUGUST 30 8:18 AM

## Hospitalized Teen Showing Signs of Recovery

There was positive news out of TriCounty Memorial Hospital last night as the condition of Edward Youngblood, age 13, was upgraded from guarded to serious.

The young football player suffered a head injury at preseason camp last Friday. Sources at the hospital report that doctors have been encouraged by Edward's progress and are cautiously optimistic that he will emerge from his coma in the next day or two.

The Youngblood family—as well as the head of the camp, Walthorne High Hall of Fame football coach Louis Bizetti—were unavailable for comment.

GUYS SO I THINK IT'S OUT

I THINK SOMEONE TOLD

I DON'T KNOW WHO

WE NEED TO STICK TOGETHER
NOW MORE THAN EVER

REMEMBER THIS TOWN LOVES FOOTBALL

PEOPLE WILL STAND BY US NO MATTER WHAT

WE JUST NEED TO STICK BY EACH OTHER

WE'RE STILL THE WALTHORNE WILDCATS

REMEMBER THAT

Tuesday at 9:57 am

**Susie** it's a new day, please everyone be kind 2 each other, think positive thoughts pleeeez we need our friend to get better.

 22

Like · Reply

Tuesday at 10:06 am

**Amanda** I love you guys.

 20

Like · Reply

MR. RASHAD:     You want some?

ETHAN:          Not really. I'm not hungry.

MR. RASHAD:     Okay great, more for me.
                So.
                I wasn't sure you would want to meet
                today.

ETHAN:          I didn't.

MR. RASHAD:     Okay, then why did your mom call?

ETHAN:          I just had, I just wanted to know what
                you . . .

MR. RASHAD:     Go on.

ETHAN:          I want to know what you know.

MR. RASHAD:     What do you mean?

ETHAN:          Come on. I know you know something,
                I could tell by the stuff you were
                asking me yesterday. And last night

I got a text from a kid who said
people are starting to figure out what
happened.

MR. RASHAD:    I thought you said you weren't reading
texts.

ETHAN:    I wasn't.

MR. RASHAD:    Okay.

ETHAN:    You're talking to other kids. I just
want to—I just want to know what
people are saying.

MR. RASHAD:    Well, I can tell you that people are
upset and shocked and on edge. I
already told you my colleagues and I
are talking to the kids who want to
talk.

ETHAN:    I don't get why—

MR. RASHAD:    Ethan, you have to understand
something. For some people, it helps
to get things off their chests. It
helps to talk about it. Even if they
did something wrong.

ETHAN:          Who said I did anything wrong? I
                didn't do anything wrong.

MR. RASHAD:     I never said you did.

ETHAN:          Then what's there to talk about? I told
                you a zillion times nothing happened.

MR. RASHAD:     But you just seemed to suggest
                something *did* happen. That your friend
                texted you—

ETHAN:          You're confusing me.

MR. RASHAD:     Okay, let's take a step back. I want
                to be straight with you. You're
                right, we're starting to hear some
                other things. We're starting to hear
                that maybe this wasn't just a simple
                football injury.

ETHAN:          What are you talking about?

MR. RASHAD:     Tell me again why you came here today?

ETHAN:          I—my parents wanted me to.

MR. RASHAD:     I talked to your parents, and they

said this was your decision. Yesterday,
you said you were done talking to me,
that there was nothing more to say. And
yet, you're here. Why?

ETHAN:        I told you. I want to know what people
              are saying.

MR. RASHAD:   Do you want to talk about what
              happened to Teddy?

ETHAN:        What?

MR. RASHAD:   Other people are starting to talk, so I
              thought maybe you were ready too.

ETHAN:        Who's starting to talk?

MR. RASHAD:   I can't tell you that right now.

ETHAN:        You said you weren't a cop, why are you
              acting like a cop—

MR. RASHAD:   If someone forced you to do something,
              you will not be in trouble, I promise
              you that.

ETHAN:        Stop asking me—

MR. RASHAD:    Okay. Okay, Ethan.
               Just one more question. Do you know
               what hazing is?

ETHAN:         Hazing?

MR. RASHAD:    That's right.

ETHAN:         No.

MR. RASHAD:    It's when a group of people initiates
               someone from the outside into their
               organization, or onto their team, by
               making them do something they might
               not want to do. It's like a ritual,
               or a tradition. Usually it's stupid.
               Sometimes it's dangerous. But people do
               it because they're desperate to belong,
               and because the ones with the power
               pressure them to do it. We're learning
               that there have been rumors of hazing in
               the football program at this high school
               over the years, but no one has ever come
               out and admitted it. We're just trying
               to find out if these reports are true,
               that's all. We're trying to see if some
               good can come out of all this.

ETHAN:          This wasn't that. We're not on the
                high school team. We haven't even
                started high school yet. This was a
                summer camp.

MR. RASHAD:     With high school kids.

ETHAN:          Yeah, I guess.

MR. RASHAD:     Tell me more about the Rookie Rumble.

ETHAN:          Why? What about it?

MR. RASHAD:     You told me it's a freshmen scrimmage
                that the seniors coach. Is that all?

ETHAN:          What?
                What do you mean?

MR. RASHAD:     I mean I've heard there's more to it
                than that.

ETHAN:          I can't—
                I don't really remember—

MR. RASHAD:     Ethan, if you don't help us, the same
                thing that happened to Teddy might

happen to someone else. Other kids are going to get hurt.

ETHAN:          I thought you said you weren't trying to get anyone in trouble.

MR. RASHAD:     I'm not. I'm just trying to protect kids like Teddy. Like you. That's all.

ETHAN:          I don't believe you.

MR. RASHAD:     Ethan—

ETHAN:          I don't believe you.

**INSIDE**

*I can't*

*I can't remember*

*What*

*How*

*After*

*Eden*

*Come on, Eden*

*Let's do this*

*Don't be soft*

*Waiting*

*Shouting*

*Me*

*You*

*Teammates*

*Brothers*

*This wasn't supposed to*

*This wasn't supposed to*

*Please*

*Please*

*You have to believe me.*

## MOM

Good morning, honey

It's really good to see you

Hey guess what, I got some rest

I feel like a person

I feel human for the first time since this all happened

Last night, I was worried I scared you when I screamed

I just couldn't believe it

You know how when you pray for something so hard

And you try to have faith but a part of you just isn't sure

And so when it happens

When you opened your eyes, if only for a few seconds

I knew it was the beginning

It's almost like a miracle

It is a miracle

So I finally slept

So that was good

And when your dad told me that Janey actually sang in the car this morning, I cried

Oops, too sappy?

No more sappiness I promise

I just want to say

I love you

And all the other stuff

The rumors or whatever

I don't know what is true and what isn't true, but I do know we'll figure it all out later

Because I honestly don't care about any of it right now

I truly don't

I just care about you

I love you.

## NANA

Well

Don't you look fresh as a daisy

Relatively speaking

I'm not going to sit here and chew your ear off, you get enough of that around here

But I just want to show you what I've been up to

Yup, that's right, I baked your favorite cookies

Take a look at these babies

How's that for cruel?

Smell that melted chocolate

Just the way you like it

Come and get it, Teddy

I got a whole plateful for you.

Just as soon as you're ready, Teddy Bear

Just as soon as you're ready.

## DAD

Can you squeeze my hand?

Oh man

Oh man that's perfect

Great job, Ted

Look at that

You're really almost back

It is so good to see you, Teddy

So so good

I almost can't believe it

We love you so much, never forget that

And Mom's right

We have heard some stories about the football camp

The team-building stuff, the bonding stuff

I called Coach Bizetti this morning to ask him

He swears he had no idea

None

I don't know

I want to believe him

He sounded stunned

Like he could barely talk

I just, I don't know, I mean, who knows what's true?

I don't want to guess

I don't want to rush to judgment or anything

We just need you to get well

The doctor is supposed to be here any second

I know she's going to want to talk to you, Teddy

I'm sure she wants to talk to all of us

Alec is here too

Maybe you want to see him

Teddy

We're all right here.


## DR. SPARKS

It's good to see you this morning, my friend

You look terrific

Do me a favor and squeeze my hand

Ah yes, great job

You're a terrific listener

So good to have you with us

Now I just want to tell you and your parents a few things

Teddy has been through a trauma

A significant trauma

Obviously his improvement has been very gratifying, but we have a long way to go

He can hear you, but he is not quite ready to speak

The important thing is for Teddy to get his rest

Stay relaxed

Breathe easy

Conversation is good but easy does it

Fun, nice, easy conversation

A few friends and family

Keep it light

Hopefully in another day or two, Teddy will be able to take a look around

And say hi to everybody

And if things continue to progress, we can remove the breathing tube once and for all

We will keep a close eye on things

A close eye on things, young man

But for now, rest

Nice, easy rest.

ETHAN

I'M AT THE HOSPITAL NOW

I'M IN THE WAITING ROOM BUT I'M GOING TO SEE TEDDY IN A LITTLE WHILE

HE'S COMING OUT OF IT AND WAS AWAKE LAST NIGHT WITH HIS EYES OPEN

ALSO I WANTED TO TELL YOU I KIND OF TALKED TO THE THERAPIST LADY ABOUT WHAT HAPPENED

I HAD TO

I'M SORRY

I DIDN'T SAY ANY NAMES THOUGH I SWEAR

SHE SAID SHE WOULD LEAVE MY NAME OUT OF IT BUT MY MOM IS ASKING ME A LOT OF QUESTIONS

IT'S LIKE SHE KNOWS SOMETHING

I WANT TO TELL TEDDY'S PARENTS BEFORE THEY FIND OUT SOME OTHER WAY

UNLESS YOU WANT TO?

IF YOU WANT TO, LET ME KNOW

TEXT ME BACK SOON THOUGH OKAY?

**DAD**

Teddy

The doctor is right

I don't think we're doing you any favors with all these visitors

I know what everyone said, stimulation is good

But it's too much

It's been way too much

So now I'm making a decision

A decision to—


**MOM**

Jim

I just talked to

Why didn't you tell me—


**DAD**

You what?

You talked to who?

Sarah, we agreed

Please don't—


## MOM

Teddy

Teddy, I know you can hear me

I know I said I don't care about that other stuff right now

And I don't want you to feel alarmed

I don't want any stress, I really don't

But I

I just got a call from Alec's mom

She said she saw his phone

His texts

There was definitely some sort of planned thing

There is a boy who hurt you

Who hurt you deliberately

This was not just about football

This was about some contest

Some disgusting contest

This was an organized

I mean I

It's almost impossible to believe but apparently it's true

Apparently the police are looking into it

The police!

This was intentional

Someone hurt you intentionally

As some sort of—

**DAD**

Sarah

You're not

What did we talk about?

Please

**MOM**

Jim

I'm just trying to protect my son

Something happened, now we know for sure

I want answers

If Teddy can tell us somehow

Give us a sign

Nod, blink his eyes, I don't care

I want to know

I want to know who did this

Who did this to our son

You might not care, but I do


**DAD**

Are you serious right now?

After you leave, after you walk out on this family

I could almost laugh, I really could

How dare you say I don't care

How dare you

I called the coach, he's coming here

He is absolutely heartbroken

He will give us answers

**MOM**

You called the coach

He's heartbroken? Please

Scared out of his mind maybe

You go ahead and call the coach

Maybe you can ask him when Teddy can play football again,
since you seem to think he can


**DAD**

I don't think that

I wasn't thinking straight

Let's go downstairs and get a cup of coffee

This is not getting us anywhere

This is not helping our son

I don't want to

Let's go.

Tuesday at 11:19 am

**Eric** I can't believe what I'm hearing. Somebody must have ratted. Somebody broke code.

Like · Reply

Tuesday at 11:28 am

**James** Whoever you are, you need to not show up at school. Seriously we will find u.

 8

Like · Reply

Tuesday at 12:02 pm

**Caleb** Shut up you guys.

👍 2

Like · Reply

Tuesday at 12:23 pm

**Amanda** Ur bullies that's what you are.

👍 6

Like · Reply

## JANEY

Teddy, hey

Um

Can you open your eyes again, like you did yesterday?

That was awesome

Are you sleeping?

I hope you didn't hear Mom and Dad

It was like after dinner in the old days, when we would be sitting in the TV room

Remember?

Covering our ears, turning the TV up to block it out

It was just like that

But is it true, Teddy?

I was with some friends who heard the same thing

Like you were beat up or something

Some kid attacked you

Is that

Do football players really do that?

Do they really beat each other up for fun?

To act cool?

Like, do kids really do that to each other?

That is like

That doesn't make sense

I don't get it

And if somebody beat you up, I'm going to beat them up

I swear I will.

**ALEC**

So hey

Teddy

Can you like

Can you like hear me right now?

This is getting crazy

It's getting real

Your parents are in the waiting area

They started asking me all sorts of questions

Your mom is like a little insane right now

Your dad was telling her to calm down

They were talking to some other guy too

One of the therapists I think

This is getting crazy

It's blowing up online

I don't know how long I have before your parents get back up here

But I wanted to tell you a couple things

It's uh

One is that I wasn't brave enough to tell people the truth

But I couldn't hold it in either

I couldn't not say anything

So I lied

I mean I told the truth but

I went online and pretended to be someone else

I mixed up the letters of my name and pretended to be some random girl named Clea

And I pretended that I'd heard rumors and knew something

So other people would want to know too and they would start talking and asking questions

I had to

And then also

Um

This therapist I've been talking to

I kind of told her too

I guess I couldn't hold it inside anymore

I didn't say anyone's name or anything

But I did tell her about the Rookie Rumble and the Hit Parade

I kind of told my mom too

It just came out after she saw some of my texts

I texted Ethan to tell him, but he's not answering

It's like he disappeared

Someone heard that he might be moving away, like to another town

That would be so crazy

All because of this

I guess his parents are, like, getting hassled or something

So they might move

I feel so bad for them, you know

But maybe it would be good, right?

If he moves?

That would be good, right?

Oh

Oh hey


**WILL**

Hey, Alex


**ALEC**

It's Alec

**WILL**

Oh sorry, man

Is it okay uh

Do you mind if I talk to Teddy for a minute?

**ALEC**

No, of course not

That's totally cool

Uh

Teddy, I'm gonna go

I'll be back later though

I promise.

**WILL**

Yo, hey, Ted

I don't

I'm pretty sure I'm not supposed to be here

I don't have a lot of time, and I don't know if you can hear me

Can you hear me?

I really hope you can

So

It turns out people are starting to ask a lot of questions

And, uh, I think it's gonna get out, what happened

But I just wanted to come by and tell you

I know you might not ever play football again, which totally sucks

But I hope you stay on the team

I hope you stick with us

People on the outside don't get it

They don't get how being on this team is the greatest thing in the world

I wish none of this had ever happened, bro, I really do

I wish it so bad

But this was an accident

A horrible terrible accident

And it's not fair if everyone gets blamed

Or everyone starts saying the whole system or everything has to change

It's not right to penalize the whole team

You think that too right, Teddy?

I know you do

You're a good kid, man, a tough kid

And I wanted to tell you too

I know I told you I thought the Rookie Rumble was so cool, and it was

But when I was a freshman and the captains told us about the Hit Parade, man we were all so nervous

At first I didn't want to do it

But

But I did it because it was tradition, you know?

We all did

And no one got hurt and it was awesome

And it reminded us that we're all in it together

And no one's ever gotten hurt like this during the Rookie Rumble

It's just so freaky, I wish so bad this didn't happen

And now people are starting to talk

I have no idea how, but it's all coming out

And it sucks for this kid Ethan

He's not a bad kid

And he loves football

But someone said he's moving away

Unbelievable

Anyway, Teddy, I should go

You're going to get out of here really soon

And I hope whatever happens, you stay a Walthorne Wildcat

Because we're the pride of Walthorne

Winning the Walthorne Way

That's who we are and what we do

You're going to walk around school and people are going to look up to you

And you're going to say to yourself, I'm a Walthorne Wildcat

Seriously, you are

And you know what? You'll be right.

**JANEY**

Hey

Uh

Excuse me

I'm pretty sure you're not supposed to be here

Who are you again?

You were here the other day

**WILL**

No, it's cool, I'm leaving

Dude

Teddy

I gotta go

Stay brave, dude

Walthorne Wildcats forever.

Tuesday at 1:12 pm

**Susie** Has anyone talked to Ethan? I heard he was talking to the cops.

Like · Reply

Tuesday at 1:42 pm

**Sammy** Ethan hasn't posted and no one has talked to him or heard from him so maybe he blabbed and now he's like hiding or something.

Like · Reply

Tuesday at 1:49 pm

**Kevin** That makes no sense why would he say something to the cops? Isn't he the one that hurt Teddy?

Like · Reply

Tuesday at 1:56 pm

**Amanda** People have tried to reach him but he's not answering.

Like · Reply

Tuesday at 2:07 pm

**Kelsey** Maybe he's on the lam from the law
#RunEthanRun

👍 5

Like · Reply

Tuesday at 2:14 pm
THIS THREAD HAS BEEN DEACTIVATED
BY THE ADMINISTRATOR.

MR. RASHAD:   Ethan, Hello.

ETHAN:   Hey.

MR. RASHAD:   I was surprised to get your call.
Usually it's your parents who call.

ETHAN:   I . . .

MR. RASHAD:   Are you okay?

ETHAN:   Yeah.
Not really.
So, are you like, a psychiatrist or
something?

MR. RASHAD:   No, I'm not. A psychiatrist is a
medical doctor. My training is as a
therapist.

ETHAN:   So you—
You can't tell me if I'm crazy?

MR. RASHAD:   I'm pretty sure you're not crazy.

ETHAN:          I think maybe I am.
                I can't sleep and I can't think and I
                can't turn off my brain.

MR. RASHAD:     I completely understand. I want to
                help you. That's what I'm here for.

ETHAN:          And it's wrong, you know? It's like,
                so stupid that I can't turn off
                my brain, and meanwhile, Teddy
                Youngblood is lying in a hospital
                and his brain isn't even working
                at all right now, like how does that
                make sense?

MR. RASHAD:     It doesn't, Ethan. But I have heard
                that Teddy is improving.

ETHAN:          Really?

MR. RASHAD:     Indeed. He's made remarkable progress
                in the last few days, which is great
                news.

ETHAN:          Oh wow. That's amazing.

MR. RASHAD:     Was there something else you wanted to
                discuss?

ETHAN:          Yeah . . . I guess people think I'm
                the one that started blabbing about
                what happened. But I'm not.

MR. RASAHD:     Well, you certainly haven't told me
                much at all.

ETHAN:          And it's not like this is the first
                time, anyway.

MR. RASHAD:     What isn't the first time?

ETHAN:          Football is a great sport, you know?
                You love it too, right?

MR. RASHAD:     I do.

ETHAN:          But it's not . . . It doesn't always
                . . . Sometimes bad stuff happens.
                Kids do stupid things I guess.

MR. RASHAD:     What kind of things?

ETHAN:          Well, they say it's for the good of
                the team. They say it brings everyone
                together.

MR. RASHAD:     You mean like bonding?

ETHAN:        I guess. But it's more like you
              have to do it, even if you don't
              want to.

MR. RASHAD:   Right. I asked you about that this
              morning. I asked you about hazing.

ETHAN:        I
              I know what happened is part of
              football, right?
              Isn't it?

MR. RASHAD:   Do you want to talk about it?

ETHAN:        I don't know. I don't—I don't know.

MR. RASHAD:   Okay. It's okay, no pressure. Maybe
              there's someone else you can talk to.

ETHAN:        Like who?

MR. RASHAD:   Have you told your parents?

ETHAN:        [INAUDIBLE]

MR. RASHAD:   Sorry?

ETHAN:        Not yet.

MR. RASHAD:     Well, maybe that's a good place to
                start?

ETHAN:          I can't. They would kill me.

MR. RASHAD:     Don't be so sure.

ETHAN:          I just wish . . .

MR. RASHAD:     Go on, Ethan.

ETHAN:          I don't know.

MR. RASHAD:     It's okay.

ETHAN:          I wish I could talk to Teddy. I
                wish I could go back in time and
                make sure none of this ever happened.
                I just—maybe that would make
                everything okay.

MR. RASHAD:     Well, one of those things isn't
                possible, as you know, but one of them
                you can do right now, if you want to.

ETHAN:          What do you mean?

MR. RASHAD:     You can't go back in time.

ETHAN:          I—huh?
                Oh.

MR. RASHAD:     You understand what I'm saying?

ETHAN:          Yeah.

MR. RASHAD:     You can't undo what happened. But
                you can deal with it, and be honest
                about it, whatever it is that you
                did, whatever happened. That can
                help you move on and figure out how
                to heal.

ETHAN:          Yeah.

MR. RASHAD:     Go home. Talk to your family. Then go
                do what you have to do. And talk to
                whomever you have to talk to.

ETHAN:          I will.

MR. RASHAD:     I was at the hospital earlier, talking
                with Teddy's parents. They are
                desperate and scared. They deserve to
                know the truth.

ETHAN:          I know.

MR. RASHAD:     Good luck.

ETHAN:          Thank you, Mr. Rashad.
                Thank you.
                Uh
                Can I ask you something?

MR. RASHAD:     Of course.

ETHAN:          Why do you love football so much?
                Especially with all this stuff going
                on?

MR. RASHAD:     That's a good question. Sometimes I
                ask myself what is wrong with me for
                loving such a violent game. Where so
                many bad things can happen.

ETHAN:          And then what?

MR. RASHAD:     I don't know. I guess the answer is
                simple—to me, it's the game itself.
                It's the most complicated and the most
                demanding game, with every player
                on a team playing a specific role and
                depending on one another. And the
                beauty of the great run or the great
                throw or the great catch or even the
                great tackle . . . it's all of it.

                    I watch it every weekend, because
                    I love it. And I know that despite
                    everything, despite all the problems,
                    I'll always love it.

ETHAN:              Yeah. I get that. Well, thanks for
                    your help, Mr. Rashad.

MR. RASHAD:         Of course. I've really enjoyed talking
                    with you.

ETHAN:              Um
                    Before I go I just wanted to say . . .
                    I know people think I'm moving away,
                    or quitting football, but that's not
                    true. I'm definitely going to play next
                    year. I'm going to play JV. I want to
                    be a Walthorne Wildcat.

MR. RASHAD:         I'm glad to hear it. And I hope we
                    can fix the system for you, and for
                    everyone who comes after you.

ETHAN:              I hope so too.

**DAD**

The coach is here

He's waiting outside

Sarah

Please don't start with him


**MOM**

Please don't start what?

I just want to hear it from his own mouth, in his own words

I want him to tell us he didn't know what was happening, he didn't know that my son was in danger

I want to hear that from him

I want him to look me in the eye and say it to my face.


**INSIDE**

*I hear you*

*I hear all of you*

*Too many*

*Too much*

*I am glad to be alive*

*I am glad you're here*

*But I miss the silence*

*This is loud*

*Everyone trying to find someone to blame*

*But sometimes no one is to blame*

*Sometimes everyone is to blame*

*Sometimes both*


**COACH**

This will only take a minute, if I may

My daughter and I just want to give Teddy a small gift

It's a game ball signed by all the guys

Before the season even starts, the first game ball of the season

We've never done this before

But we wanted to do it for you

We believe in you

Camille, did you want to say something?

**CAMILLE**

Hey, Teddy

Uh

I know I look terrible

And uh

I need to know if it's true

What kids are saying


**COACH**

Oh

Not now, honey

Honey, please—


**CAMILLE**

Teddy, did someone really do this to you?

Someone hurt you on purpose?

It can't be true, right?

I know you can't answer me right now, but I need to know

People make stuff like this up all the time

People just want to gossip and spread rumors

Everyone says they want you to get better, and they do

But also people want to make trouble

They want to make stuff up

That's just—

## MOM

Okay, uh yes, would you

Thank you for the ball

But that is not

I agree with your daughter

We just need to know the truth, Coach Bizetti

I would like to hear the truth.

## COACH

The truth

The truth is I love these boys

I'm starting to hear things that are making me sick to my stomach

And I promise you as soon as this is over

We will stop at nothing to find out exactly what happened


**MOM**

So you're saying you still don't know what happened?

That's what you're saying?

You don't know?

Isn't this your camp?

Your team?

I find that—


**DAD**

Thank you, Coach, for stopping by

It means a lot

But we should probably

It's not a great time for visitors right now

**MOM**

Yes, everybody out

Everybody out

PLEASE

Teddy, I didn't

This is

I don't mean to yell

Oh no

Please don't cry, Camille

It's not

It's not your fault, sweetheart


**COACH**

Mrs. Youngblood, please

We are here to support your son

We are here because we care

People are calling our sport and our program destructive

Calling us animals

Barbarians

But I came to support my player

Your son

So please

There is no need to raise your voice.



**DAD**

Okay

Okay

Please everyone stop

We cannot have—

Teddy?

Teddy?

What's happening?

What's happening!

Teddy?

Teddy?

Sarah

I need to go get somebody

Sarah

We need to go get somebody now.

**INSIDE**

*Where is the silence*

*I need the silence*


**NURSE RICKY**

Okay

Okay now

The doctor is on her way

She'll be right here

I need to ask everyone to stop raising their voices

Give Teddy some peace and quiet

Please

Thank you.


**INSIDE**

*Eden*

*Who is Eden?*

*Where is Eden?*

*Don't be soft*

*Don't do it*

*Do it*

*Don't*


## MOM

Where is the doctor?

My son needs a doctor


## NURSE RICKY

I know

I understand, Ms. Youngblood

I know you're upset

The doctor is on her way

I'm going to have to clear the room

Thank you all for understanding

I'm going to have to clear the room

Clear the room please.

**MOM**

I'm not going anywhere

I'm not

I'm not going anywhere until I see the doctor.


**INSIDE**

*Loud*

*Why*

*Please*

*Not*


**DAD**

Sarah


**MOM**

No

No

This is your fault, Jim

This is your fault for letting him play

Not just letting him play, but encouraging him

Loving every second of it

Even though I said no, your mother said no

You loved it

You loved watching him play this violent stupid game

**DAD**

I'm not even going to dignify that with a response

Who walked out on this family?

Who left because she couldn't handle it anymore?

Who left because the pressure was too much?

Who walked out?

**DR. SPARKS**

Everyone, please

That is not helping to say the least

Let's all take a deep breath

Teddy's heart rate is accelerating but he is stable

Teddy is okay

He is trying to tell you something

His body is doing what his brain is not quite ready to do

He is telling you to stop

The yelling

The fighting

The blaming

This is what he is reacting to

There is plenty of time for everything

To find out what happened

But not now

So please, everyone, let's calm down

Let's calm down so he can calm down.


**MOM**

I want something done

I want Teddy moved to another hospital

I don't think he's getting the care he needs here

I appreciate what you're doing, Doctor, but I'm not convinced
this is the best place for him

223

**DAD**

Sarah, please

Be reasonable

We can't have this discussion in front of Teddy

We need to go outside

Let's go



**MOM**

I want to speak to someone else

I want to speak with a different doctor

I want to find out about moving to a hospital in the city



**DAD**

This isn't how you make up for lost time, Sarah

That's not how it works



**MOM**

How dare you

**DR. SPARKS**

Please

Both of you, please

Fine, Ms. Youngblood

If that's what you want, you can come to my office

I will make some calls

We all want to do the right thing here

We all want your son to get better

I need to ask everyone to step outside

Please step outside

Thank you


**CAMILLE**

Dad

Dad let's go

I don't want to be here

I'll come back, Teddy

I'll be back to see you

I promise

**INSIDE**

*Don't be soft*

*Hit someone*

*Hit someone*


**COACH**

Perhaps we shouldn't have come today

My daughter is friends with your son

They're friends

But I'm not sure what the right thing to do is anymore


**MOM**

This isn't about you doing the right thing

This is about our son


**DAD**

Sarah

**MOM**

I want to leave this hospital

I want better care

**JANEY**

Everyone please stop

Please stop

**DAD**

I can't

**MOM**

I don't

**DR. SPARKS**

Can we all please step outside

Let's go outside

**DAD**

I'm trying

I'm trying to—

## CAMILLE

Ethan?

**MOM**

Who is this?

Who are you?

**CAMILLE**

Ethan

What are you doing here?

**DAD**

What's going on

Who are you

Is this

**COACH**

Young man, are you sure you want to—

**MOM**

Wait

Oh

Oh my God


**INSIDE**

*What*

*What is happening*

**MRS. METZGER**

Hello

I'm Ann Metzger

Ethan's mom

I

This is incredibly difficult

I've been praying for your son

Ethan is

He's been suffering

I know, it's nothing compared to what you and your son are
going through

But he wanted to come here to be with you

To help everyone understand

To help everyone heal.

**MOM**

Is your son the one?

The one responsible?

And now you're here to help everyone heal?

My son is lying unconscious in a hospital bed

And your son needs to heal?


**DAD**

Sarah, that's not—


**MRS. METZGER**

I know

I understand

Truly

I can't even imagine

I really can't

I—


**ETHAN**

Mom

It's okay, I can talk

I

Mr. and Mrs. Youngblood

I wanted to see how Teddy was doing

I was talking to Mr. Rashad

And together we decided I should come

I wasn't sure

The police have been to our house

The truth is going to come out eventually

It's already happening

People are starting to say things

Kids are saying stuff online

Stuff that's not true

It's crazy

But no one knows the full

The real truth

Mr. Rashad told me you can't go back in time

You can't relive the past

But you can't run from it either

So I wanted to come here and tell everyone the truth

The truth about what happened

Because it was

Yes

I did it

I hurt Teddy

But it was

It's complicated

It wasn't anyone's fault

It was something that just

It just happened

Something that went wrong

Really wrong

I wanted to come see Teddy

I wanted to tell him it was okay

I wanted to make sure he knew what happened was okay

It wasn't his fault either.

**MOM**

What

Let me get this straight

You wanted to tell Teddy it was okay?

That it wasn't his fault?

You hurt him

You're the one that put him in the hospital

You nearly killed him

But you wanted to tell him it wasn't his fault?


**DAD**

I have to say

I don't understand that either

I don't understand that at all

Why did you come here?


**MRS. METZGER**

Mr. and Mrs. Youngblood, please


**ETHAN**

I don't

Mr. and Mrs. Youngblood

You don't know

**DAD**

What don't we know?

What is it we don't know?

**MOM**

Hold on

Fine

I want to hear this

Jim

It's okay

Let's hear what he has to say.

**ETHAN**

Hey, Teddy

It's me

Ethan

So

I wanted to

I want to talk to you about what happened

I just need a sip of

I guess I'm nervous

So anyway

Uh

Yeah


**MRS. METZGER**

Take your time, honey

Take your time.

**ETHAN**

Okay

Okay

So

Everyone kept talking about how it was too hot for football. The sun was pounding and everyone was dripping sweat and cursing that we were out there, but it wasn't a choice. If you were an incoming freshman and wanted to play football in high school, you had to go, everyone had to go to preseason camp. We were in full pads and helmets, and a couple of times I thought I was going to throw up. At first it wasn't that bad, but later in the week it got so hot that even the coaches said we could take breaks if we needed to. But no one listened to them because we knew they didn't mean it. If you took a break, the coaches and the other kids would think you were soft. You can't be soft in football because then no one will respect you and you might not get to play. Everybody knows that.

**INSIDE**

*Show me you can hit somebody*

**ETHAN**

So even if you didn't feel good or you felt like you were going to

totally lose it, you had to suck it up and keep going. The older
kids kept telling us it builds character. They thought it was
funny when we complained about being hot or tired or sore.
They tried to scare us by saying that in high school, it gets really
intense. I guess that's true because the high school coaches
are really tough. Like hyper and scary and a little crazy to tell
you the truth. Not Coach Bizetti but all the other coaches, the
assistant coaches. Coach Bizetti seemed like the nicest one
but he never told the other coaches to knock it off. And they
would curse and say gross things sometimes and call us names
and things and some words that I never heard before but the
high school kids didn't even seem to care. They thought it was
funny. I guess they were used to it and had heard it all before.

Then on Wednesday, I got hit really hard and my arm killed, so
I skipped a tackling drill while the trainer gave me some ice.
One of the assistant coaches noticed and asked what I was
doing. When I told him my arm hurt, he yelled at me and said
that smaller kids like me need to be tougher than everyone
else. I said I would go back in as soon as it stopped stinging,
and then the same coach called me a girl and asked if I wanted
to wear a dress to camp the next day. A lot of people thought
that was hilarious and started laughing and I almost lost it
but somehow made myself not. I wanted to play so bad, and
even though my arm really hurt I needed to stay on the field,
because if I left the field then people would think I was soft or
a quitter, which is the total worst thing you can be. And I was
scared people would think I was a baby. So I went back in but it
hurt like crazy.

## INSIDE

*I love the game*

*I love running to daylight*

*I love getting hit*

*It hurts so bad*

*And it's the greatest feeling in the world*


## ETHAN

So like I said, that was Wednesday, I think, and that night I went home and my parents asked what was wrong because I guess I was pretty quiet, and I said my arm hurt a little but I was fine. So the next day was Thursday, which was the first really hot day, like it was brutal. During morning stretching, people were laughing about how the coach had called me a girl, even a few of the coaches were laughing, and then some of the older kids started calling me Eden instead of Ethan and they thought it was hilarious. And then some of my friends started doing it too. Teddy, you didn't do it at first, but then at the end of camp on Thursday, we were running laps and I was in the back, and you yelled, "Come on, Eden, don't be soft, get up here!" And everyone thought that was hilarious because you're obviously like the best football player in our grade and everyone laughs at all your jokes even if they're not that funny. So then I ran harder and caught up to you guys but it was so hot and I was really tired, and at the end of laps I couldn't really feel my legs and I fell down on the track and everyone thought that was hilarious too. The only person I saw who wasn't laughing was Alec.

But anyway, on Thursday night I made up my mind that Friday was going to be the best day of camp and I was going to show everyone what a good football player I was.

**MRS. METZGER**

Are you okay, honey?

Do you want some more water?

**ETHAN**

No I'm fine thanks

Friday ended up being the hottest day of the week, remember? By nine in the morning it was already so gross out and everyone was miserable and no one wanted to be there but the coaches still made us practice in pads and helmets because they said it's always hot at the beginning of the season and we had to get used to it. So anyway, during morning stretching one of the varsity captains, this kid Will, announces to everyone that at the end of the day we were going to play in the Rookie Rumble, which was a big Walthorne tradition where the freshmen kids play against each other in a full-pads scrimmage, and the seniors are the coaches.

*Squirts*

*Punks*

*You ready to be part of Walthorne Wildcat football*

## ETHAN

And then Will looks around to make sure the coaches aren't listening, and they're not because they're over on the main field setting up for drills. Then Will says that every year during the Rookie Rumble, they do what's called the Hit Parade, which is how they welcome incoming freshmen onto the team. And the way the Hit Parade works is that every freshman has to hit at least one other freshman so hard during the game that they have trouble getting up. We all laughed like he was joking but Will says, "I'm not kidding. This is real. You guys need to learn how to hit, and it starts today. You lay someone out so they can barely get up, you get yourself a sweet treat. And we'll tell the coaches how tough you are too." And then he says they're going to give prizes for the three biggest hits in the Hit Parade. Third prize is a steak dinner. Second prize is a case of beer. First prize is a Walthorne High School football helmet with HIT PARADE CHAMPION written on it. Will told us he had his first prize helmet on his trophy shelf at home, and he said winning the Hit Parade was one of the proudest moments of his life. Then he walked over to me and said, "Don't you want something to be proud of, Eden? You don't want to hit like a girl all your life, do you?" And everyone was staring at me so I said, "No, I don't."

**INSIDE**

*There is nothing better than being on the team*

*You will never work harder*

*You will never feel closer*

*You will never be prouder*

*This is what life is*

*Life is football*

*Football is life*

**ETHAN**

So we had the last morning of camp, and I actually did really well. I made some nice plays and the coach who'd called me a girl even smacked me on the shoulder pads once and said good job, said I was a tough kid. I think maybe he felt bad for calling me a girl on Wednesday. I know I'm not nearly the biggest or best player or anything, but I'm a good football player and it felt really good to have the coaches say nice things about me. So then after lunch, since it was the last day of camp, the coaches gathered us all in a circle and Coach Bizetti gave a pep talk about the upcoming season where he said football was like war in peacetime, and a team is a band of brothers, warriors on the battlefield and we're all in it together and if one person loses his focus we all suffer and then everyone yelled and screamed and cheered and it was the loudest noise I'd ever heard in my life.

It was kind of awesome actually. And then the coaches pulled the freshmen aside and told us to go off and have fun with the Rookie Rumble—they would be keeping an eye on us but the seniors were going to do the coaching, and that they would be getting reports from the seniors on which of us would make true Walthorne Wildcats some day.

I'll

I'll take that drink of water now, please

Thanks

So before the game starts, they break us into offense and defense. Teddy, you were playing tailback of course. I'm at outside linebacker. The game starts and we're hitting pretty hard, but the seniors are screaming at us like, "Come on! This is pathetic! You're a bunch of old ladies!" and other stuff way worse than that. They're yelling from the sideline the whole time. "You want to be one of us? You want to be tough, don't you? You want to be part of the team, don't you? Hit somebody! Hit hard! Hit hard!" And then Will calls us all over and starts yelling about the Walthorne Wildcats tradition and the poster that's on the locker room wall, about winning the Walthorne way and how "No one is alone on the team" and "No one is bigger than the team" and "We work together, we fight together, we protect one another, we defend one another," stuff like that, and everyone started chanting "No one is bigger than the team" over and over, and yelling "No one!" And Will screams, "Who wants the beer? Who wants the steak? Who wants the freakin' helmet?" except he used curse words. And we all start yelling, "I do! I do! I do!"

## INSIDE

*These are your brothers*

*Your fellow warriors*

*I've waited all my life for this*

## ETHAN

And when we start playing again, everyone is hitting much harder, and after one play where you ran over some kid, one of the seniors yells, "Young Teddy Youngblood is turning into a full-grown man!" and everybody thinks it's hilarious. It's getting super intense, but for some reason I start to lose my focus. I think about the fact that everybody called me Eden the day before, and how weird it is that if you hit someone so hard they can't get up, then you get a prize, and it just all starts to feel wrong to me and so I lose my focus like I said, and on the next play I totally get crushed by Alec, I mean just leveled, and all the seniors come over to Alec while I'm still on the ground, smacking him on the back and yelling at me like "Eden! Eden get up! Get up you little girl! Get up old lady!" and Alec looked like he was about to help me up, but then Teddy, you run over right then and you high-five Alec while I'm lying there

And

And Teddy I know you didn't really mean it, but you were yelling too, you were calling me Eden again too, but I was still a little wobbly from the hit, and I was still on the ground, so you yelled, "Get up! Don't be a girl! Don't be soft! Come on, Eden, let's do this!"

## INSIDE

*Don't be soft*

*Come on Eden let's do this*

*Let's do this Eden*

## ETHAN

Everyone was fired up, kids were laughing, even a couple of the coaches were laughing. I don't think they knew exactly what was going on, but they saw how excited everyone was and they loved it

And finally I got up and I looked at you, and what you were doing just didn't seem like you, and I felt my eyes and ears start to buzz and I think I know what they mean when they say you start to see red because I felt this anger start to form in my body like it wanted to burst out of me

And so I pushed everyone out of the way and went back to the huddle and suddenly the only thing I cared about was showing everyone how tough I was, showing you all I wasn't soft, and just because I was small didn't mean I couldn't hit as hard as anyone else

But I didn't say a word

And the next play was a run to our left side. Teddy you had the ball, and I was playing right outside linebacker so I had to run all the way across the field, and by the time I got there you were wrapped up—kids were trying to tackle you but you wouldn't go down because you're so strong

And three guys had you around the legs and the waist but you were still standing straight up, and your head was like the only part of you that wasn't wrapped up

## INSIDE

*Darkness inside the light*

*Thoughts but no words*

## ETHAN

And I was running full speed with the buzzing still in my ears, the angry red buzzing

And then you stopped struggling because the play was basically over, but I was still running as hard as I could, sprinting, I couldn't stop

I was so mad because of all the insults and people calling me Eden and calling me soft and calling me a girl

And I couldn't take it anymore

And you could feel me coming and your head turned in my direction and I could see your eyes through your face mask, they went really wide in your head

And I jumped

Like I launched myself at you

And I hit you full on

Helmet to helmet

I was like a missile and you were the target and I heard a sound when I hit you

It was like, CRACK!

Really loud


**INSIDE**

*I'm falling*

*I'm falling*

*I'm*

## ETHAN

And I could feel the breath kind of leave your body as you fell to the ground and everyone froze and no one said anything for a few seconds, and then the first thing I heard was somebody go "Holy crap!" and then someone else said "That was a late hit!" A few of the seniors ran out onto the field and Will screamed at me that it was a cheap shot. And it was. I knew it was. And right away the anger drained out of my body, and I got really scared. I couldn't move, nobody moved—we were all watching you, and after a few seconds you got up and it was like we could all breathe again, because you seemed okay. You looked at me but didn't say anything. I could see that your eyes were foggy, but you went back to the huddle and one of the coaches came over to make sure you were okay and you said you were but I could tell something was wrong but somehow you managed to keep playing. It was so hot but we kept playing for about ten more minutes, and anyway nobody really hit each other that hard after that, even the senior boys seemed a little scared after I hit you, but we finished the game, and right then, it started to rain

We finished the game and we were heading to the sideline when I first saw you wobble

We were walking across the track and you were weaving back and forth

Alec was the first to reach you

He asked if you were okay and you said, "Yeah, fine."

And because you're so strong and such a good athlete, everyone believed you

We all believed you, Teddy

And then you said, "Is it raining?"

Which was the last thing you said

And then I heard you make a noise, like a moan, and then you fell

And there was another noise when your head hit the track, like a thud

A noise I never heard before, but now I hear it all night

Now I can't stop hearing it

Everything stopped and I saw you lying there on the ground

At first I thought maybe you were just tired or dehydrated because it was so hot, but you didn't move

Your eyes were closed

And I heard some kid say, "Oh my god"

And another kid said, "Somebody get the coach"

And some kids ran away

And Will looked at me and said, "What the hell did you do?"

And then he screamed it again in my face, "WHAT THE HELL DID YOU DO?!"

And I just stood there

And I didn't know where I was

And I didn't know what was happening

And more kids ran away

And some kids stood there

And it started to rain harder

And a few seconds later some of the coaches came running up and before anyone said anything, Will said, "Teddy just collapsed or fell or something, I think he hit his head." And Coach Bizetti looked at everyone and he looked at me and it seemed like maybe he didn't understand what was happening, but he didn't ask anybody any questions either. All he did was kneel down and look at Teddy and he took out his phone and called 911 and the other coaches came running over too and told the high school kids to go to the locker room and the freshmen kids to go up to the parking lot and wait for our parents and Will came up to me and said, "You know what happens now, right?" and I just stared at him until he said it again, really softly, "You know what happens now, right?" and I could tell everyone was staring at me, so finally I nodded, and he said, "Good"

And then he leaned in really close to me and said, "Not a word about the Hit Parade, or the prizes, or anything. Not a word. To anyone. Ever."

Then he went into the locker room with the other varsity kids, and all the incoming freshmen were still standing there like we were all afraid to move, and no one said anything and no one made a sound, and then I heard someone crying and I think

I think it was me.

**INSIDE**

*Light*

*Circles*

*Colors*

*Almost there*

*Almost here.*

**MRS. METZGER**

It's okay, honey

It's

It's okay

It's okay.


**DAD**

I uh

Thank you

This is a lot

I'm sure you've been through so much

I appreciate that you came here

That took courage

These are

There are so many different ways to look at something

But

I'm sure you may not be remembering everything correctly

Or you may be remembering some things and not others

I don't

It's not possible that Teddy would do those things

Would act that way

He's a good kid

A great kid

I'm sure there's more we need to know

But thank you for coming forward.


## MOM

He's being nice

My husband

My ex-husband

He's being too nice as usual

I know you've been through a lot, Ethan

I understand you were in shock

Probably still in shock

But I have to say

That does not give you the right to come here

After having injured my child

To tell us this—

This story

You make it sound like it was his fault

His fault?

His fault that he almost got killed?

That you almost killed him?

Ethan, I need to ask you and your mother to leave

You shouldn't be here

I don't want my son seeing you

After all this

You did this to him

Why should anyone believe you

We were just starting to hear someone did this to him

I mean, don't get me wrong

I'm sure that everything you're saying about the coaches' attitudes and the stuff about seniors urging freshmen to injure each other is one hundred percent true

That doesn't surprise me at all, in fact

But saying that Teddy provoked you

That you're the victim?

That this was some kind of

That everyone ganged up on you

That's convenient

Why hasn't anyone told us this before?

Why should we believe you?

## INSIDE

*I was there*

## DAD

Sarah

Sarah, please

## ETHAN

I

Mrs. Youngblood I didn't mean to make you upset

## MOM

But you did

You did make me upset

Everyone and everything is upset

Look at what's happened now

Teddy is uncomfortable

The pillow is still not right


**DAD**

Sarah

You need to

Enough


**MOM**

The pillow is all wrong

This boy hurt my Teddy

He's dangerous


**MRS. METZGER**

Please do not

Please do not talk to my son that way

**ETHAN**

I

You should talk to the other kids

They can tell you

Coach, tell them

The coaches might not have been watching closely

But they must have known

I don't know if they knew everything

But they must have known something

Tell them, Coach.


**COACH**

I

This is very

I had no idea

Of course I knew there was some silly stuff involved with the Rookie Rumble

Seniors having fun with the freshmen, welcoming them to the team

It happens everywhere

But this is the first I've heard of the Hit Parade

This is the opposite of what I teach these kids

This is all

I had no idea

All we wanted to do was create unity

A team

A family that would do anything for each other

Go to battle together

These kids are like sons to me

I love them as my own kids

This is my life

This is not what I teach

I had no idea

The last few days, I'd heard some things

I didn't know what to believe

It sounded so crazy

I started hearing some things

But I didn't want it to be a distraction

There is only one thing to think about and that is praying for your son's recovery

Of course we will address it after your son recovers

I've been waiting because I didn't want to cause more pain
right now

I just want your son to get better

But it was going to be addressed

We were going to deal with it

Fix it

There's so much good that this program does

Being part of something special

Teaching boys how to grow up

Be strong

How to look out for themselves

How to build the friendships that form on that field

Bonds that last a lifetime

Those are—


**DAD**

Coach Bizetti

I'm sure you feel badly, and I appreciate that

And yes

Maybe it's true you didn't know exactly what was happening

But isn't it your job to know?

Isn't it your job to lead and to do the right thing?

You're in the Hall of Fame

You're a legend in this town

But none of that matters anymore

You're more concerned with protecting your reputation than protecting our kids

You had me fooled

I trusted you and I believed in you

You know what?

It turns out you're no better than anyone else.


**MOM**

Mr. Bizetti, it's possible that you care about the kids and have a good heart

But my guess is that you care about winning more

You failed my son and the other kids and the whole town

You failed to protect our children

You and your coaches watched and laughed

And if you didn't know, it's because you didn't want to know.

**DAD**

Thank you for coming, but I think you should go

Coach Bizetti

You need to go now.


**COACH**

I

Yes

I will be in touch of course

I am praying for Teddy

Goodbye.

GUYS

I KNOW I SAID WE NEED TO STICK TOGETHER AS A TEAM

IT'S MORE IMPORTANT NOW THAN EVER

TEDDY IS AN AMAZING KID AND HE'S GOING TO BE OKAY

I DON'T THINK HE'LL PLAY FOOTBALL AGAIN BUT HE'LL ALWAYS BE A WALTHORNE WILDCAT

WE'RE NOT GOING TO LET ONE LAME CHEAP SHOT BRING US DOWN

WE STAY STRONG

LIKE IT SAYS ON THE LOCKER ROOM WALL

NO ONE COMES BETWEEN YOU AND THE TEAM

WE ARE WALTHORNE

NOW ON TO BUSINESS

EVERYONE KNOWS OFFICIAL PRACTICE IS SUSPENDED

BUT WE ARE HOLDING CAPTAIN'S PRACTICES

HELMETS NO PADS

LET'S GET BACK AT IT

TEAM MEETING FIRST THING TOMORROW
MORNING, 8AM AT THE FIELD

DON'T BE LATE

**ALEC**

Hey

I'm

Hey


**DAD**

Alec?

What are you doing here?

This isn't a good—


**ALEC**

I

I had to come back

I heard Ethan was coming

Ethan

I hope you're

Did you

Did you tell them?

**ETHAN**

I told them.

**ALEC**

Everything?

**ETHAN**

I

I

**MOM**

Alec, is it true what he told us?

About what happened?

**ALEC**

I uh

I wanted to be here when Ethan told you

I lie awake at night thinking about hitting Ethan during the
Rookie Rumble and then celebrating

High-fiving other kids while Ethan was lying there

While you were lying there, Ethan

Not helping you up

It keeps me up at night

That's not me, I swear it isn't

I don't

I don't think I want to play football anymore.

**DAD**

Thank you, Alec

It took a lot of courage for you to come here.

**MOM**

Oh, Alec

You're Teddy's best friend

Why did this happen?

How could you all let this happen?

**JANEY**

Mommy

Dad

Please

You shouldn't blame Ethan

Or Alec

Or anyone

It wasn't anyone's fault

They were just

Ethan was just

It's not his fault

Ethan, I think you're brave

You didn't have to do this

You didn't have to come

You didn't have to admit anything to anyone

You're really

You're just really brave.


**ETHAN**

I really

Thank you, Janey

And

I don't

Mr. and Mrs. Youngblood

I hope you can forgive me

I don't

It isn't anyone's fault

This is just what happens with sports and teams and stuff

Sometimes it gets crazy

And so much of it is great

But sometimes it gets crazy

I wish it didn't have to be like that

I still love football

I still want to play

Maybe it will be different now

Maybe things can change.


**ALEC**

Maybe

I hope they can

**INSIDE**

*I'm getting ready*

*I'm almost there*


**DAD**

Sarah, do you hear these kids?

They're right

We need to take into account what we've done

And you're right, I got too wrapped up in it

Maybe I didn't look hard enough at what was really going on

And when Teddy hit someone hard, I loved it

I cheered louder than anyone else

I was so proud of him

I was

I loved it

That's all there is to it

I loved it.

**MOM**

Jim

I don't mean to

I'm just so tired

But I know how much you've done for our kids

And I know how hard it's been for you

Teddy

Janey

Can you

Can you forgive me?


**DAD**

We'll find a way

Teddy

Janey

We'll always be here

I promise you

We will always be here for you.

**MOM**

Yes

Yes we will.

**INSIDE**

*I'm ready*

*I'm ready now*

**JANEY**

Teddy

Can I hold your hand?

Think of home

Think of your bed

Think of Ollie licking your feet

Think of fried chicken

Think of Chinese food

Just feel my hand holding your hand.

**MOM**

Ethan

I hope you know

I didn't mean

I shouldn't have spoken to you like that

I hope you understand what we are going through

But that is not an excuse

You're right

This is not your fault

I'm just so exhausted

But you're absolutely right

And, Janey and Alec, you're right

Things have to change

We need to make sure things change.


**INSIDE**

*I see the colors*

*I have the words*

*I'm ready*

**JANEY**

Oh

Teddy, did you just do that on purpose?

Teddy just squeezed my hand

I think

Teddy just squeezed

Wait


**DAD**

He

He squeezed Mom's hand before

He is starting to respond

I wouldn't get—


**JANEY**

This seems different

Wait

See?

He did it again

Teddy?

Teddy?

Mom, look

Dad

Teddy?


## MOM

What's happening

Oh my God

Get the

Teddy?

Get the doctor

Teddy's waking up

Teddy, honey

Teddy

It's mommy

I'm right here

I'm right

Jim, go get the doctor

I'm right here, honey

Teddy, I'm right here

I'm not going anywhere

I'm right here

Oh my—

Wow

Look at your big, beautiful eyes

That's right

You're safe

You're here with us

Janey is here

Dad is getting the doctor

We're right here

Hi, honey

It's really good to see you

It's so good to see you, honey.


**NURSE RICKY**

Whoa Whoa Whoa

What do we have here

Look at this

Good morning

It's morning in America, people

Let me just get in here for a second

Check a few things

Good

Good

Better than good

The doctor is coming

The doctor will be right here

You just relax

It's good to see you, young man.


**DR. SPARKS**

Well

What is happening?

All sorts of good stuff I see

This is a sight for sore eyes

Hello, Teddy

We haven't been formally introduced

I'm Dr. Sparks

Let me just see here

Look into my light, okay, Teddy?

Look left

Look right

Up

Down

You see how many fingers I'm holding up?

Can you hold up the same number of fingers with your right hand?

Now with your left?

That's great

That's perfect

You've had a good rest, a nice long rest

Good to have you back with us

I'm going to ask the nurse to help me here

This is not going to hurt one bit

You are not even going to feel a thing

We are going to take out this tube

Your throat will feel a little dry

You might cough a bit

It's not going to feel great

But it won't hurt

Talking is going to take some time

But we've got plenty of that

Nurse, please help me here

That's it

Yep

Yes

Terrific

There we go

You're doing great, Teddy

You're doing terrific.


## MOM

Thank you, Dr. Sparks

You've been so wonderful

I hope you know I didn't mean what I said earlier

You've been amazing

Oh my God

Teddy

This is such a blessing

Jim

Teddy is pointing

He's asking for water

Dr. Sparks, he can drink?

Please, Jim, can you

Thank you

Here we go

Use the straw

There you go

That's it, honey

Small sips

Janey

Janey, he wants to hold your hand

Honey, Janey was holding your hand when you woke up

She's got the lucky hands

Okay

Daddy is going to sit here

I'm going to get some ice chips

I'll be right back

I'll be right here.

**DAD**

Hey, kiddo

Hey

This is what we've prayed for

Everyone has been praying for this moment

And now our prayers have been answered

It almost doesn't seem real to have you back

I was

I'm not going to lie, I was a little worried there

A little scared

I mean

I know what a tough kid you are

But I was scared

I love you so much, Teddy

Remember I said you were a game changer

This time you really are

You're changing the game for keeps

I'm so proud of you, son.

**MOM**

Jim

Jim, wait

I think Teddy might be trying to tell us something

Ethan?

Ethan and Alec, come over here

Okay, honey

I just don't

We don't want you to do too much


**ALEC**

Hey, buddy

Hey

Man it's good to see you

It's

Oh man

I'm just

Wow

I'm so glad to see you.

**ETHAN**

Hey, Teddy

Hey

I

It's uh

I'm so glad to see you too

Everyone is

I'm really happy to see you

**DAD**

Teddy

Everything is okay now

**MOM**

Go ahead, Teddy

Honey, go ahead

What is it you want to tell us?

**TEDDY**

I remember.

# Young Athlete Emerges from Coma; Investigation on Cause Will Be Launched

A lot of local prayers were answered today as officials at TriCounty Memorial Hospital confirmed that Edward Youngblood, the young football player who was injured last Friday at preseason camp, has emerged from his coma and is expected to make a full recovery.

The family was unavailable for comment, but Coach Louis Bizetti released a prepared statement through the high school. "The entire Walthorne Wildcat community is totally thrilled and delighted at the news of Teddy's improvement," the statement read. "The Youngbloods are a wonderful family, and our hearts have gone out to all of them over these last difficult days. We wish only the very best to the family, and a return to full strength for Teddy, who is such a tough kid. We're dedicating our season to this terrific young man."

In other developments related to this case, there have been reports of a dispute about what exactly caused the young student's injury, with some online commentary suggesting that a hazing ritual may have played a role.

"I can't confirm any of the details related to this particular situation, and I urge the public not to jump to conclusions," said Board of Education spokesperson Celia Cutliffe. "What I can tell you is that there will be a full investigation, and depending on the results, we will implement changes that need to be made in a careful and thorough manner."

More on this story as it develops.

# AUTHOR'S NOTE

I love football and I always have.

I didn't play—back in the day, my go-to sport was soccer—but when I was a kid, the NFL was pretty much my favorite thing to watch on TV. I was a huge Jets fan, and still am—I have no idea why, since they're almost always lousy—but I'll watch any football game if it's good.

When my youngest son, Jack, was in seventh grade, he announced to our family that he wanted to switch from soccer to football. My wife, Cathy, wasn't crazy about the idea, but I was fine with it. In fact, I was excited. This was about ten years ago, and the long-term dangers of concussions were just starting to become well-known, but I didn't think too much about that. These were kids, after all. How hard could they hit?

Well, pretty hard, as it turned out.

My son ended up playing through high school, and he was pretty good. He got knocked around a lot, but luckily, no major injuries. The friendships he formed with his teammates last to this day. The coaches seemed tough but fair. And there was no obvious hazing—at least none that I was aware of.

But as time went on, I became aware of a few things. One, sports may be the only organized activity in this country where adults can scream and curse at kids and it's not only okay but expected. Two, as the world gets more competitive, the world of sports gets more competitive too, especially the world of youth sports. Three, the injury scare is real at any age—several of my son's teammates gave up the game because they got too many concussions. And four, younger kids will do anything—and I mean, anything—to impress their older teammates and feel like they belong.

Oh, and five, watching Jack's high school games are some of my favorite memories as a parent. It turns out football is a hard habit to break.

*Game Changer* is a work of fiction. It does not reflect what I saw, only what I know is out there. And it's up to adults to keep kids as safe as possible, even when allowing them to play a violent sport.

It's the least we can do!

# FOR MORE INFORMATION

There is a ton of information about youth sports, safety, and hazing on the internet. Here are just a few articles I found interesting while doing my research:

"Is football safe for kids? Study looks at brain changes"
www.today.com/news/football-safe-kids-study-looks
-brain-changes-t104222

"NFL Commissioner Roger Goodell to reluctant football parents: We're making the game safer"
www.today.com/news/nfl-commissioner-roger-goodell
-reluctant-football-parents-we-re-making-t102819

"Alleged Hazing Leads To Cancellation Of Remainder of Middle School's Football Season"
www. newyork.cbslocal.com/2012/11/28/alleged-hazing-leads-to
-cancellation-of-remainer-of-middle-schools-football-season/

"Despite Greater Awareness, Violent Hazing Still A Problem In School Sports"
www.forbes.com/sites/bobcook/2013/09/09/despite-greater

-awareness-violent-hazing-still-a-problem-in-school-
sports/#1224b999275a

"Youth football concussion and safety awareness for 2017"
youth1.com/football/youth-football-concussion-safety
-awareness-2017

"Long Island Football Player Dies After Being Hit by 400-Pound
Log"
www.nytimes.com/2017/08/12/nyregion/long-island-football
-player-dies.html

More articles surely have been published since this book went to
print, so please check online for the latest news.

# ACKNOWLEDGMENTS

Thanks to Brianne Johnson for helping me find the right editor.

To Erica Finkel for helping me tell the right story.

To Dr. Jonathan Greenwald for giving me the right medical advice.

To the team at Abrams/Amulet for making the right decisions.

And to my family for being the right family.

COMING SOON FROM TOMMY GREENWALD:

# *RIVALS*

## THE THRILLING COMPANION NOVEL TO *GAME CHANGER!*

## READ ON FOR A SNEAK PEEK.

# RIVALS

When it comes
to winning,
nothing's out
of bounds.

# TOMMY GREENWALD

*You know what's weird?*

*When you're falling through the air, about to crash into a hard wooden floor and get really badly hurt or possibly die, you have a lot of time to think.*

*Which is good, because I have a ton of stuff to think about as I fall.*

*The first thing I think is, this isn't as scary as I thought. I mean, it's definitely scary, but it's also calm.*

*And silent.*

*Like, the world stops.*

*I keep falling, and I keep thinking.*

*I think about everything that led up to this moment.*

*I think about my mom and dad.*

*I think about not wanting to die.*

*I think about how much it's going to hurt when I land, if I don't die.*

*I think about what kind of injuries I'm going to have and how long it will take for me to get better.*

*I think about how the injuries might be so bad, I won't be able to play basketball again for a long time. Or ever. Or maybe I'll be able to play, but I won't be as good as I am right now.*

*And I think about how that might not be the worst thing in the world.*

*I hit the floor.*

*I hear a* SLAM! *Then a* CRACK!

*And everything goes dark.*

# FIRST HALF
## Four Months Earlier

**PROWLING WITH THE PANTHERS**
A MIDDLE SCHOOL SPORTS BLOG BY ALFIE JENKS
MONDAY, NOVEMBER 5

## Hoops Season Kicks Off with Middle-School Tradition

You can feel the crispness in the air. You can try to ignore the holiday commercials popping up on television, and you can hear the rustle of winter coats being removed from mothballed closets all over town.

That can only mean one thing: it's basketball season in Walthorne!

This is a town that takes its basketball extremely seriously; four Walthorne hometown heroes have made it to the NBA over the years and one to the WNBA, while many student-athletes have received Division I scholarships. Girls and boys all over town are getting ready for the season at every level, from the district champ Walthorne Wildcats high school team right down to the kindergarten Superkitten League.

One tradition that everyone looks forward to is the season-opening game between the Walthorne North Middle School Cougars and the Walthorne South Middle School Panthers. Since 1986, these two rivals have played each other twice a year: the first game of the season and the last game of the season. And it's always an exciting, fun-filled event.

I caught up with key members of each team as they were practicing for the big game. Austin Chambers, fourteen, is the captain of the Walthorne North squad. A point guard, Austin is the son of Frank Chambers, local legend and former star shooting guard at Penn State. "This is going to be our year," Austin told us. "We've got a strong team and a great bunch of guys. Keep an eye out for Clay Elkind, our center. He's turning into a huge weapon for us." Across town, fourteen-year-old Carter Haswell, a young phenom who already stands six feet one inch tall and was all-state last year as a seventh grader, captains the Walthorne South squad. "I think we could go far," said Carter. "I like our chances a lot, and Benny Walters is the best coach in the league. But Walthorne North is always tough, and they'll be a great first challenge for us."

These two young men will lead their teams onto the floor this Friday at Walthorne South gym. Game time is 4 pm. (And just a personal note: I will be broadcasting the game LIVE on our middle school radio station and website! So feel free to tune in.)

WWMS
WALTHORNE SOUTH RADIO


ALFIE:          Testing, testing 123 . . .
                Is this thing on?


CARTER:         If you're talking to me, I can't
                hear you.


ALFIE:          Dang it! This equipment is pretty old.
                Mr. Rashad said he was trying to get
                us some new stuff but he uh . . . so,
                yeah, sorry, hold on a sec . . . how
                about now?


CARTER:         Oh sweet, now I got you. Yup,
                we're good.


ALFIE:          Cool. (BANGS THE MIC)
                Okay, so, yeah! Welcome to Talking
                Sports on WWMS. It's Wednesday,
                November 7th, and my name is
                Alfie Jenks, sports editor and
                head sportswriter.


CARTER:         So, will anyone actually, like,
                hear this?


ALFIE:          What do you mean?

CARTER:     Like, does anyone listen to your show?

ALFIE:      Oh absolutely.

CARTER:     Like who?

ALFIE:      I mean, well, you know, it's mostly
            just for fun and stuff, but like, I
            think my mom definitely listens.

CARTER:     (LAUGHS) HA! Cool. Well in that case,
            I'll try not to swear.

ALFIE:      Thank you.

CARTER:     What kind of name is Alfie for a
            girl, anyway?

ALFIE:      I'm named after my grandfather. I like
            it. Why, you don't like it?

CARTER:     Uh, no, it's cool.

ALFIE:      I think so, too. So, anyway, yeah,
            once again welcome to the show
            everybody. That voice you hear
            belongs to Carter Haswell, eighth
            grade basketball star and captain of

the Walthorne South Middle School
Panthers. We're here to talk about the
upcoming game, the first game of the
season against your archrivals, the
Walthorne North Cougars. Carter, what
are your thoughts?

CARTER:     Uh, my thoughts?

ALFIE:      Yeah. You know, like, your thoughts
            about the game and stuff.

CARTER:     My thoughts. Got it. Well, my thoughts
            are that I hope we win.

ALFIE:      Cool.

CARTER:     Cool.

ALFIE:      Everyone's been looking forward to
            this game since the end of last year,
            when the two teams battled it out for
            the league championship and you guys
            beat them in the finals by three.

CARTER:     That was pretty awesome, especially
            winning in that fancy new gym
            they built.

ALFIE:      Yeah. I wonder when we're gonna get a
            gym like that.

CARTER:     Probably never.

ALFIE:      So now it's a new season, though, and
            Walthorne North has a lot of tall
            players, especially their center, Clay
            Elkind. What's the plan to contain
            them? Are you gonna play zone, maybe
            a box and one, or do you think you
            can handle them playing man-to-
            man? Are you concerned about their
            pick-and-roll?

CARTER:     Whoa. You know a lot about basketball.
            Like, more than me even.

ALFIE:      I love basketball.

CARTER:     Cool. I like basketball, too.

ALFIE:      Do you love it?

CARTER:     Uh, sure, I guess. I'm not, like,
            obsessed with it or anything.

ALFIE:      That's so weird because people are
            saying you're, like, one of the

best players to ever come out of
Walthorne, and you're not even in
high school yet.

CARTER:     I don't pay attention to any of that
            stuff. A lot of people take basketball
            too seriously if you ask me. I mean,
            it's just a game, right?

ALFIE:      If you say so. So if you don't take it
            seriously, how did you get so good? Do
            you practice a lot?

CARTER:     I practice when I feel like practicing,
            which is a lot, but, like it's not all
            I ever do. Do you play an instrument?

ALFIE:      No.

CARTER:     Oh. Well, I love playing guitar, but
            I'm way worse at that than I am at
            basketball. It's like, some things
            you're really good at, and some things
            you're not, and that's just the way it
            is, you know? With basketball, people
            tell me I have a feel for the game. I
            guess that's part of it.

ALFIE:      Plus you're tall and super athletic.

CARTER:        Yeah well, that's all luck.

ALFIE:         I guess so. Well, it's almost time for
               next class, so thanks for coming on
               the show.

CARTER:        No problem.

ALFIE:         Oh wait! I almost forgot, the school
               asked me to announce that the town is
               doing this online pep rally thing, and
               they want us to encourage people to
               go on there and say supportive things
               about all our sports teams and show
               some school spirit!

CARTER:        Oh yeah, I heard about that. I
               guess that sounds fun, so yeah, for
               whoever's listening out there, check
               it out—wait, what's it called again?

ALFIE:         Walthornespirit.com

CARTER:        Right yeah, Walthornespirit.com. I
               guess, like, lots of kids are going
               to be on there getting psyched up
               for the winter sports season, so
               all the boys and girls teams are

counting on everyone for support and
stuff. Thanks.

ALFIE:          Thank <u>you</u>, Carter! This has been
                Alfie Jenks, Talking Sports. Be sure
                to tune in next week, when my guest
                will be seventh grade gymnastics star
                Rebecca Smythe.

# CHECK OUT *RIVALS*, COMING SPRING 2021!